D0459512

STRANGE PLANET: THE SNEAKING, HIDING, VIBRATING CREATURE

PRINTED IN THE UNITED STATES OF AMERICA.
 FOR INFORMATION ADDRESS HARPERCOLLINS CHILDREN'S BOOKS, A DIVISION OF HARPERCOLLINS PUBLISHERS, 195 BROADWAY, NEW YORK, NY 10007.

WWW.HARPERCOLLINSCHILDRENS.COM

ISBN 978-0-06-304974-1

THE ARTIST USED PROCREATE TO CREATE THE DIGITAL ILLUSTRATIONS FOR THIS BOOK.

TYPOGRAPHY BY NATHAN W. PYLE

21 22 23 24 25 PC 10 9 8 7 6 5 4 3 2

❖

FIRST EDITION

STRANGE PLANET

THE SNEAKING, HIDING, VIBRATING CREATURE

NATHAN W PYLE

HARPER
An Imprint of HarperCollins Publishers

TO OUR YOUNG BEING.
WELCOME TO OUR
STRANGE PLANET.
WE ADORE YOU.
♡

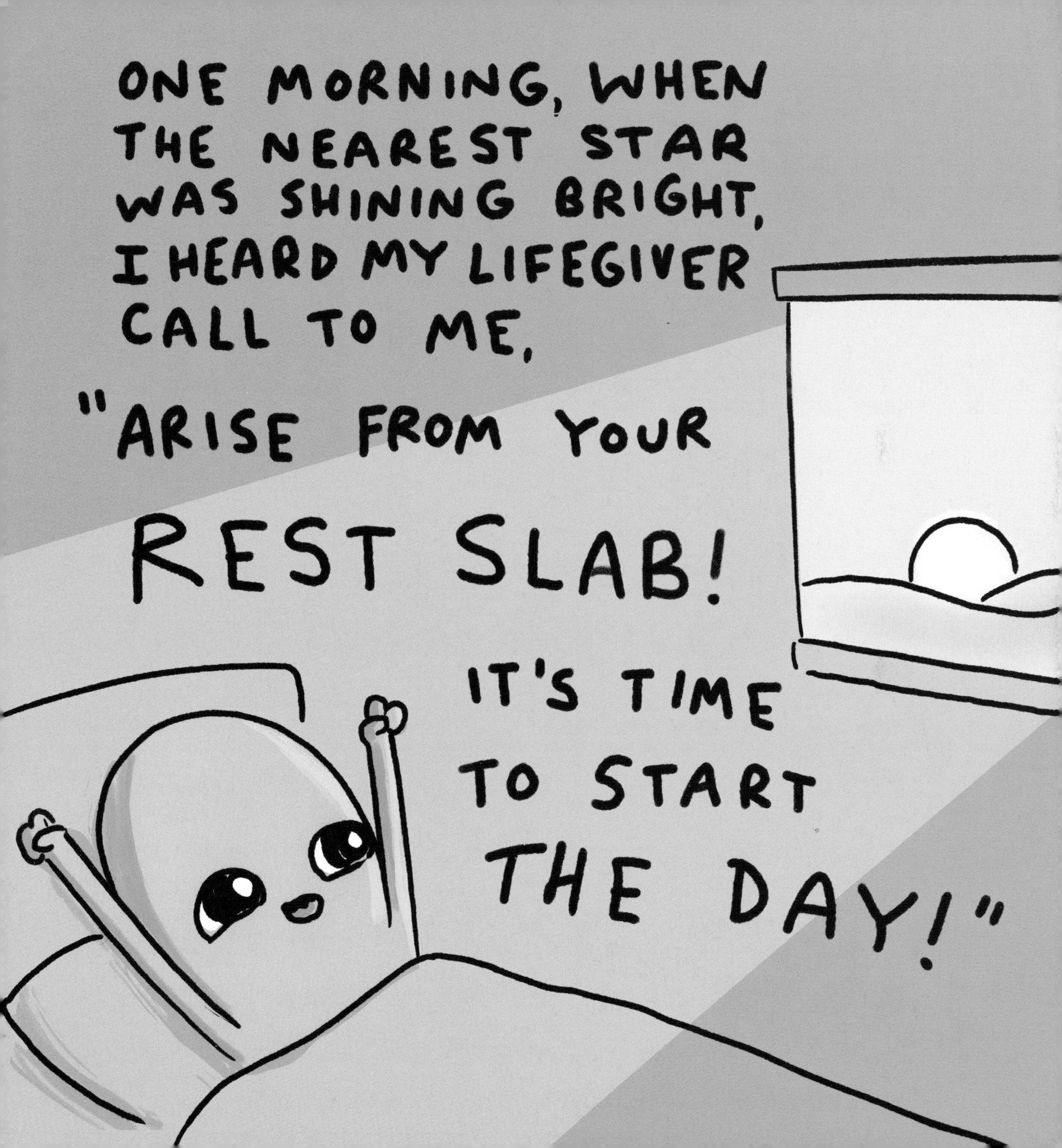
ONE MORNING, WHEN THE NEAREST STAR WAS SHINING BRIGHT, I HEARD MY LIFEGIVER CALL TO ME,
"ARISE FROM YOUR REST SLAB! IT'S TIME TO START THE DAY!"

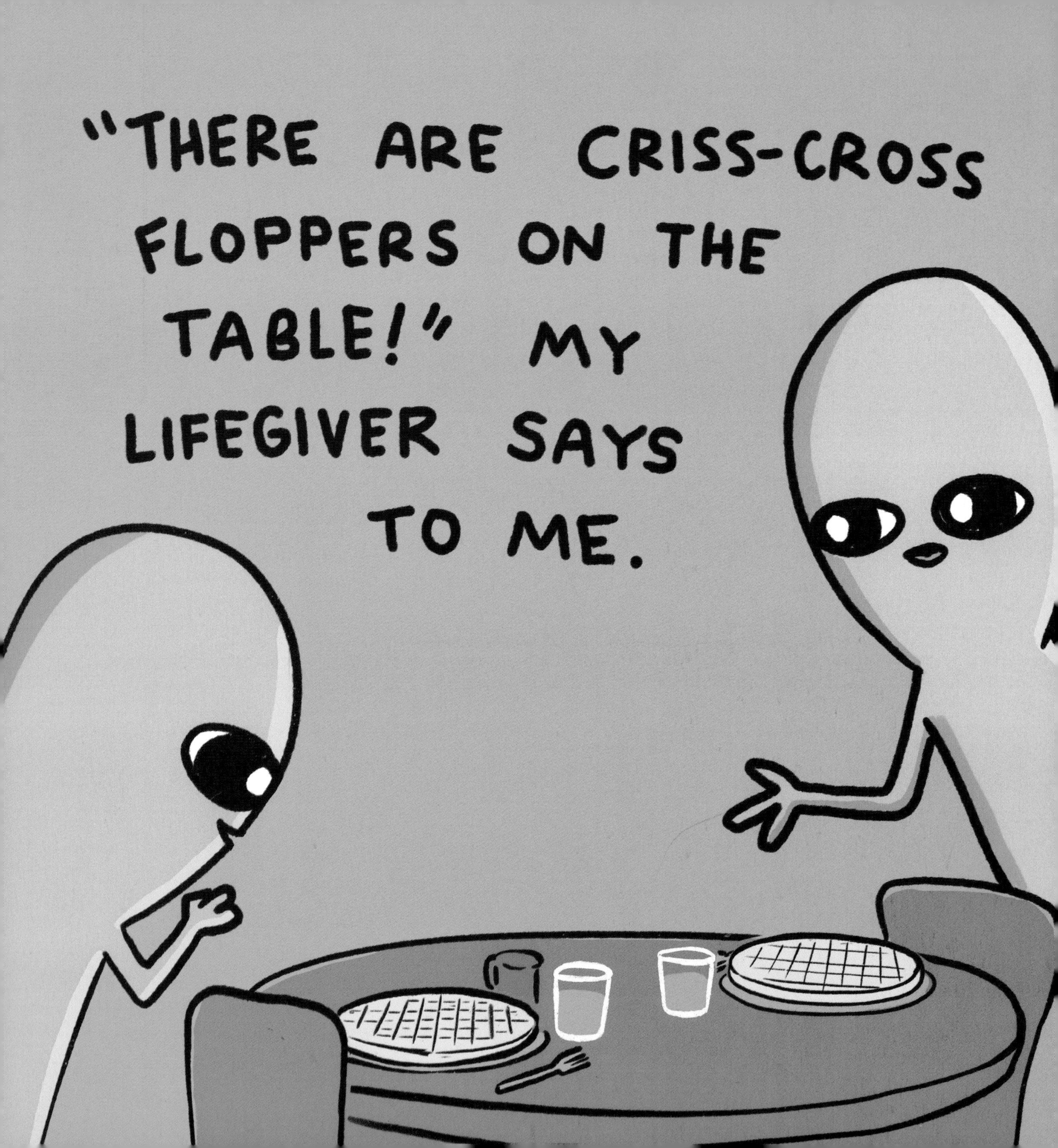
"THERE ARE CRISS-CROSS FLOPPERS ON THE TABLE!" MY LIFEGIVER SAYS TO ME.

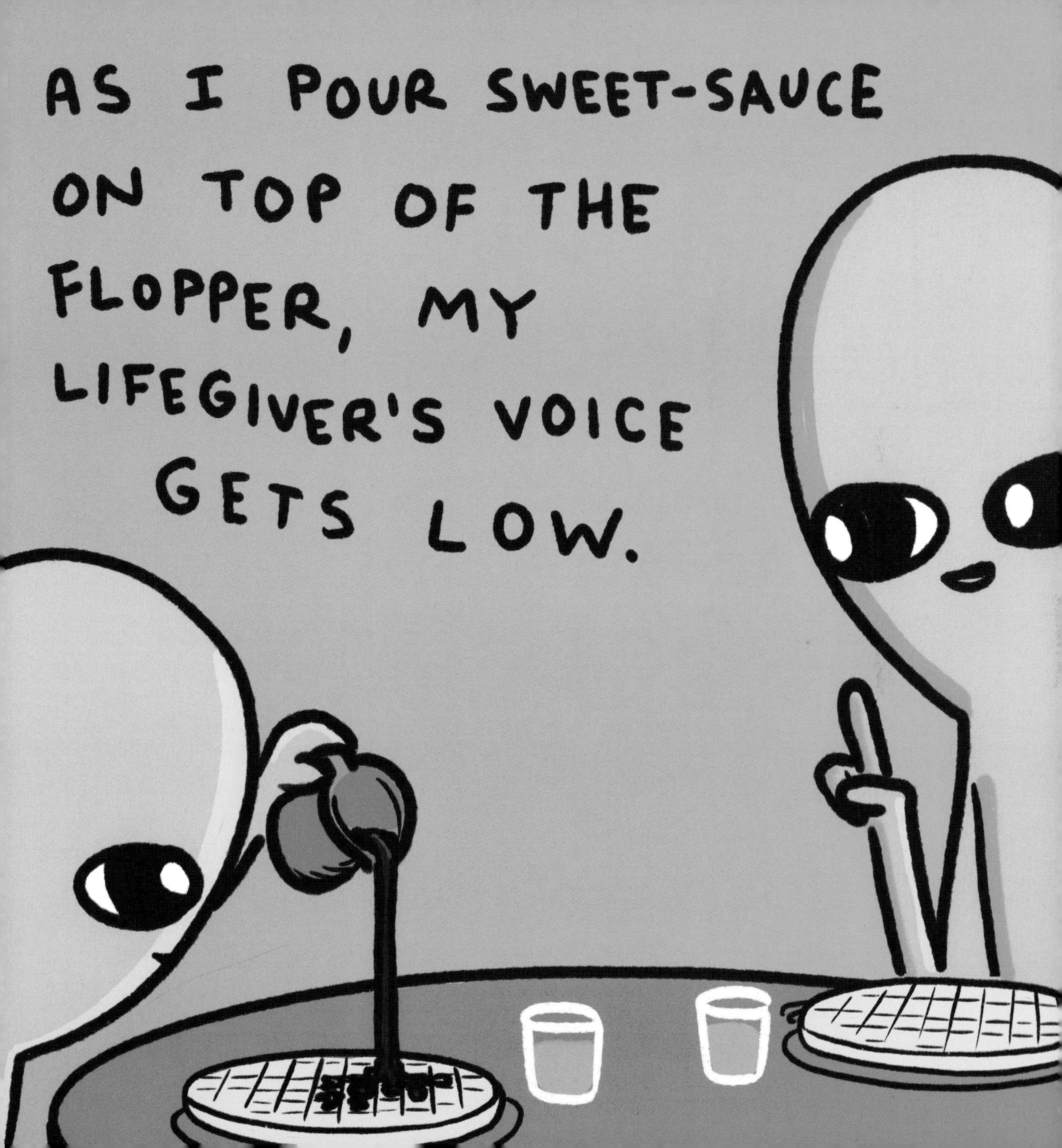
AS I POUR SWEET-SAUCE ON TOP OF THE FLOPPER, MY LIFEGIVER'S VOICE GETS LOW.

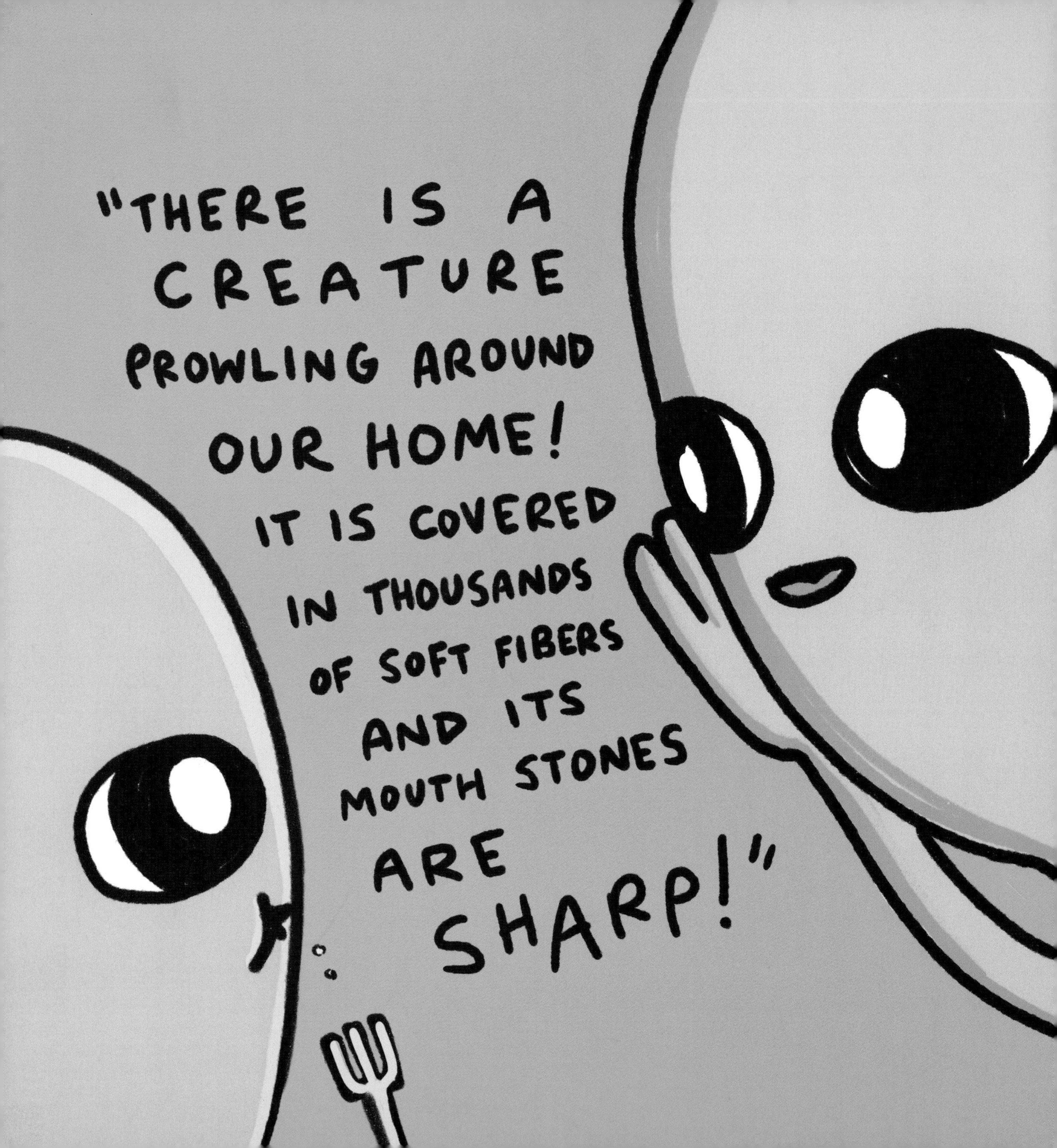
"THERE IS A CREATURE PROWLING AROUND OUR HOME! IT IS COVERED IN THOUSANDS OF SOFT FIBERS AND ITS MOUTH STONES ARE SHARP!"

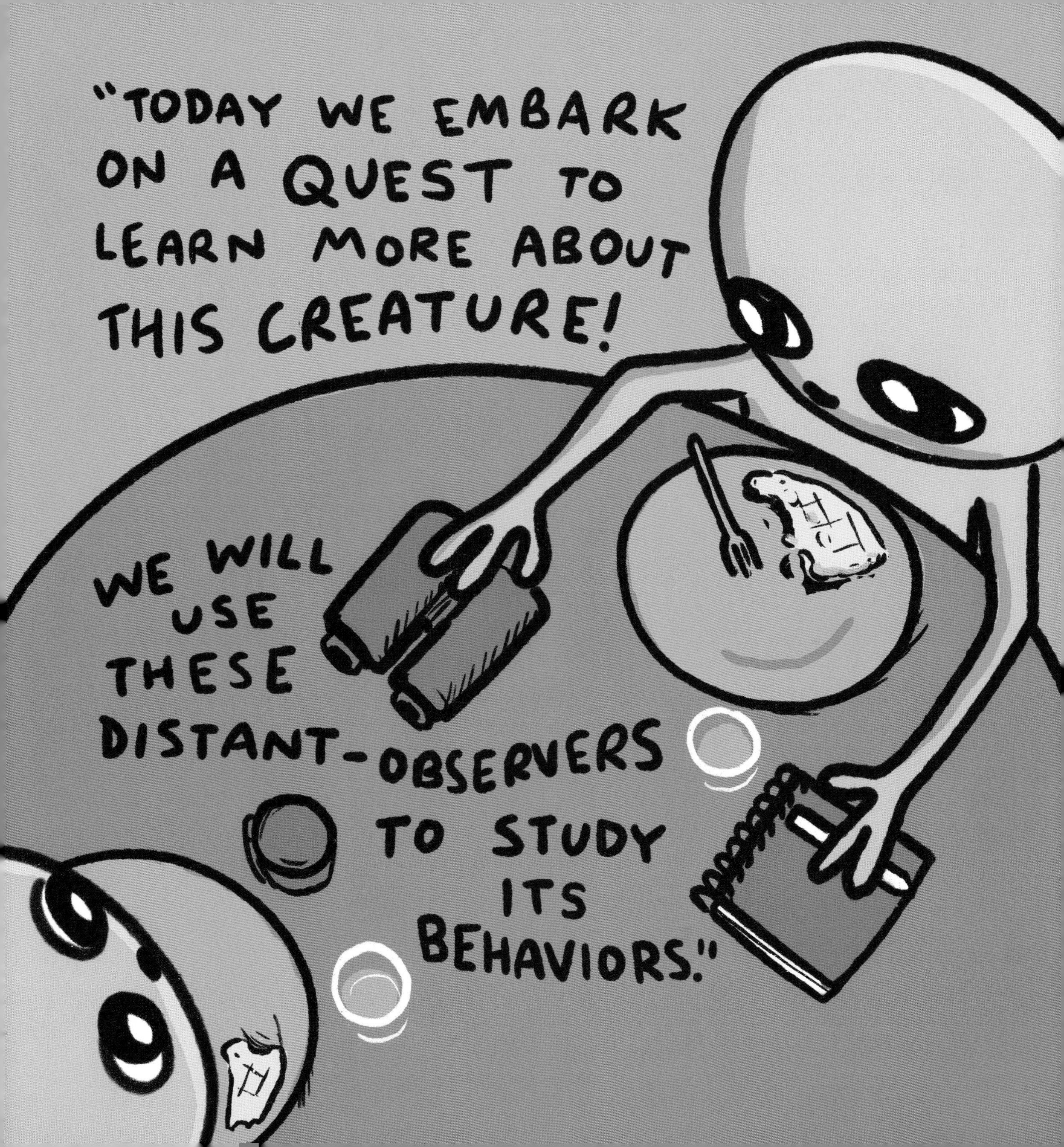
"TODAY WE EMBARK ON A QUEST TO LEARN MORE ABOUT THIS CREATURE!
WE WILL USE THESE DISTANT-OBSERVERS TO STUDY ITS BEHAVIORS."

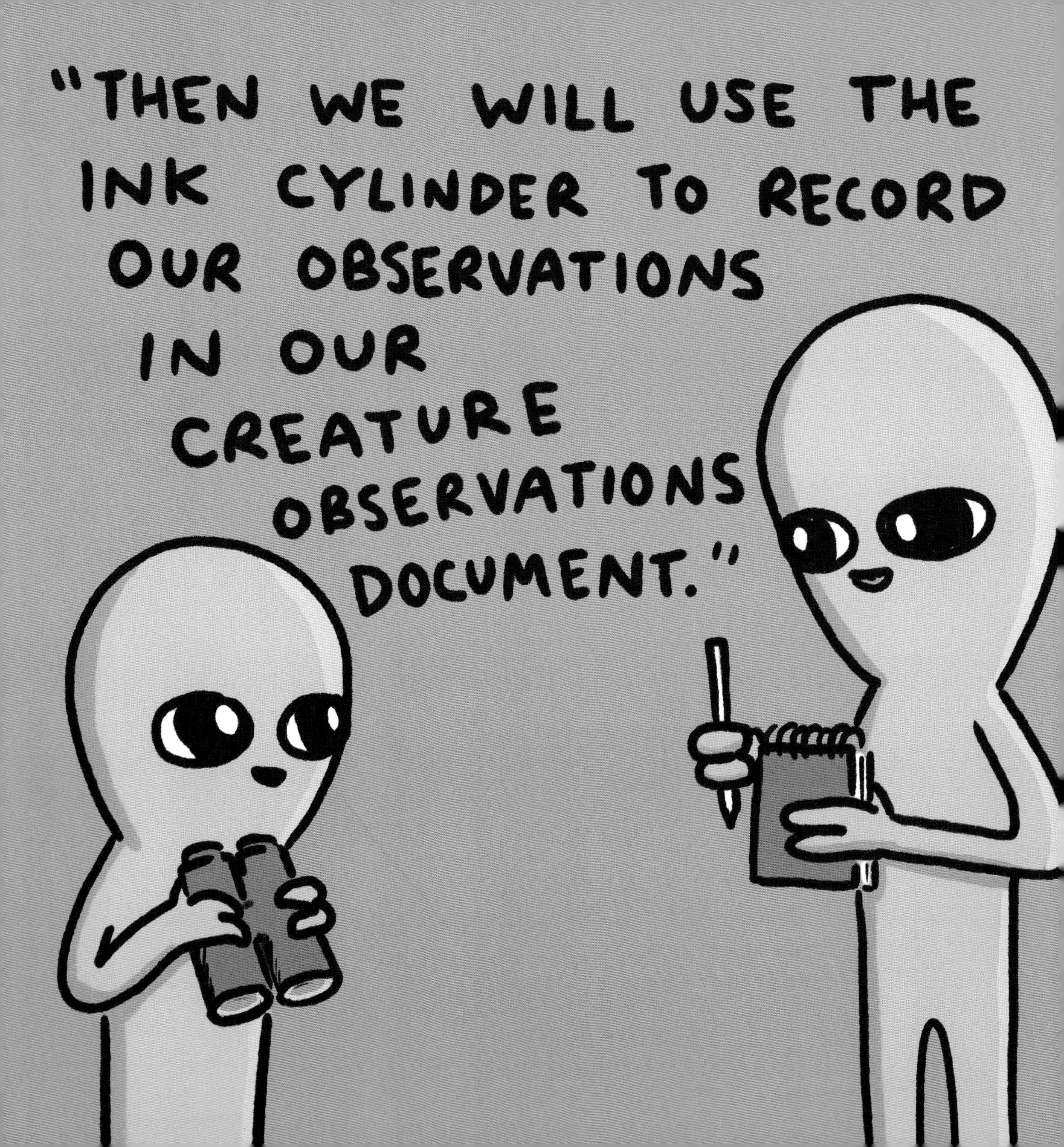
"THEN WE WILL USE THE INK CYLINDER TO RECORD OUR OBSERVATIONS IN OUR CREATURE OBSERVATIONS DOCUMENT."

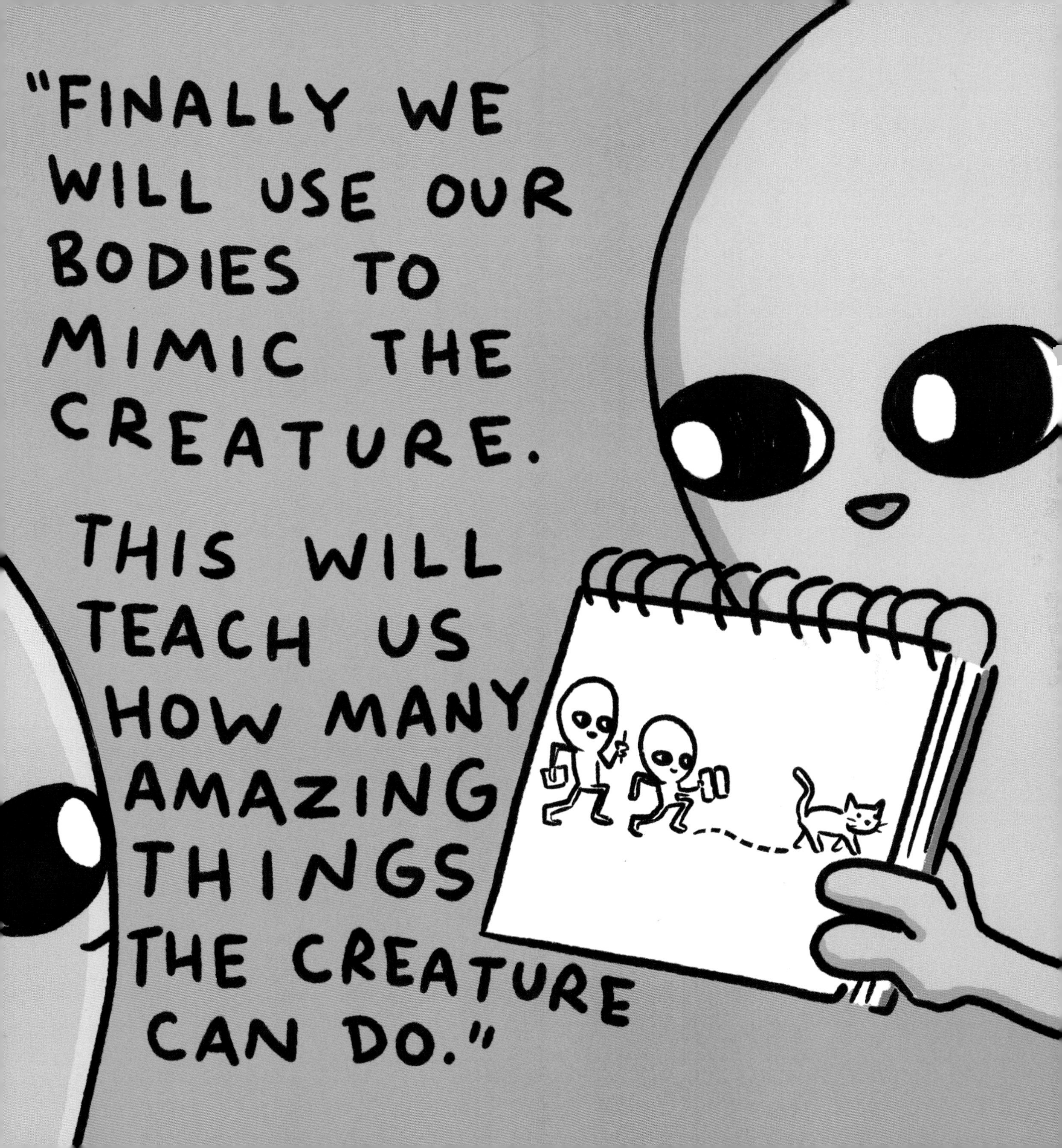
"FINALLY WE WILL USE OUR BODIES TO MIMIC THE CREATURE.
THIS WILL TEACH US HOW MANY AMAZING THINGS THE CREATURE CAN DO."

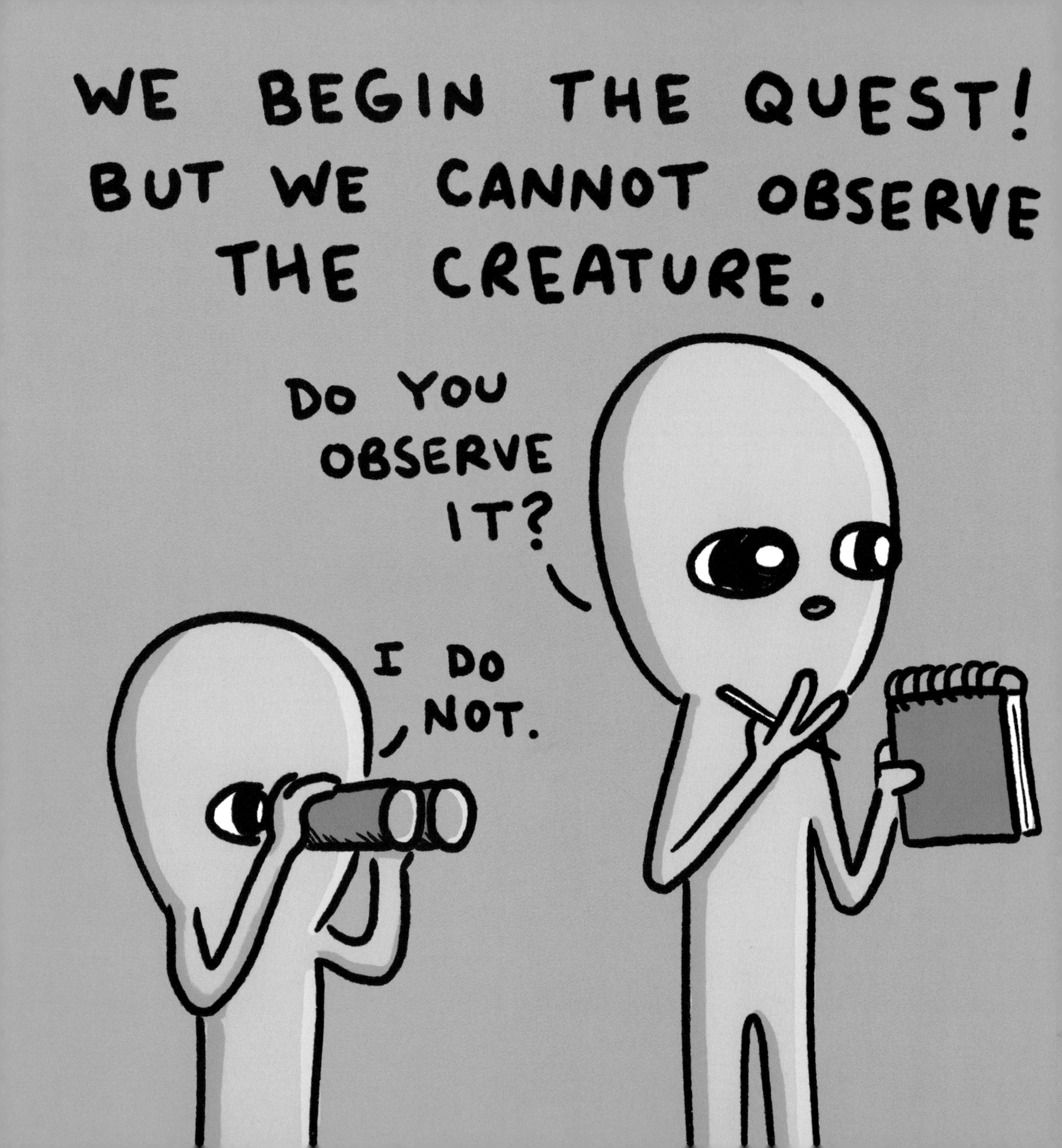
WE BEGIN THE QUEST! BUT WE CANNOT OBSERVE THE CREATURE.
DO YOU OBSERVE IT?
I DO NOT.

"WHERE IS IT?" WE ASK, AND SEARCH ALL AROUND US.

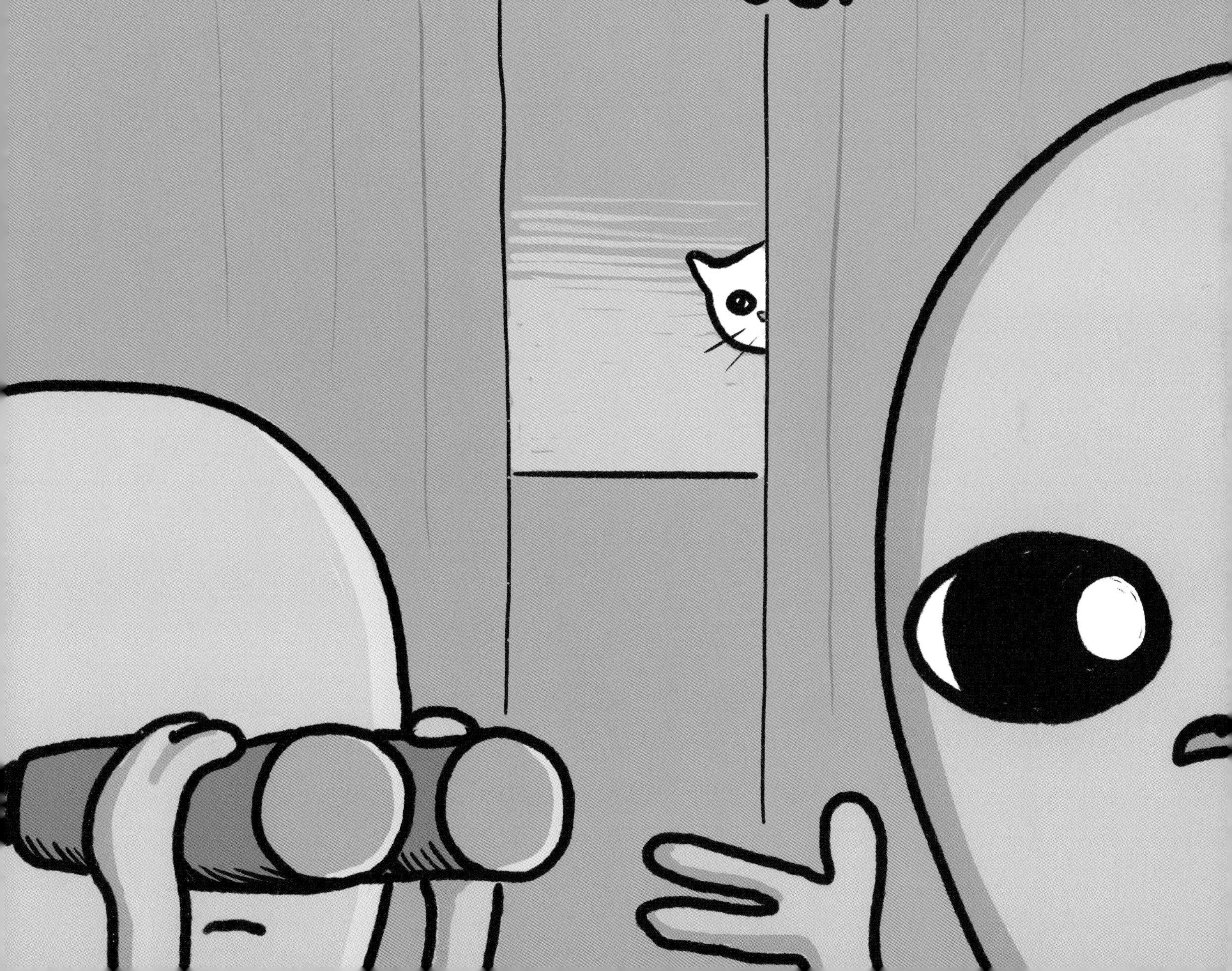

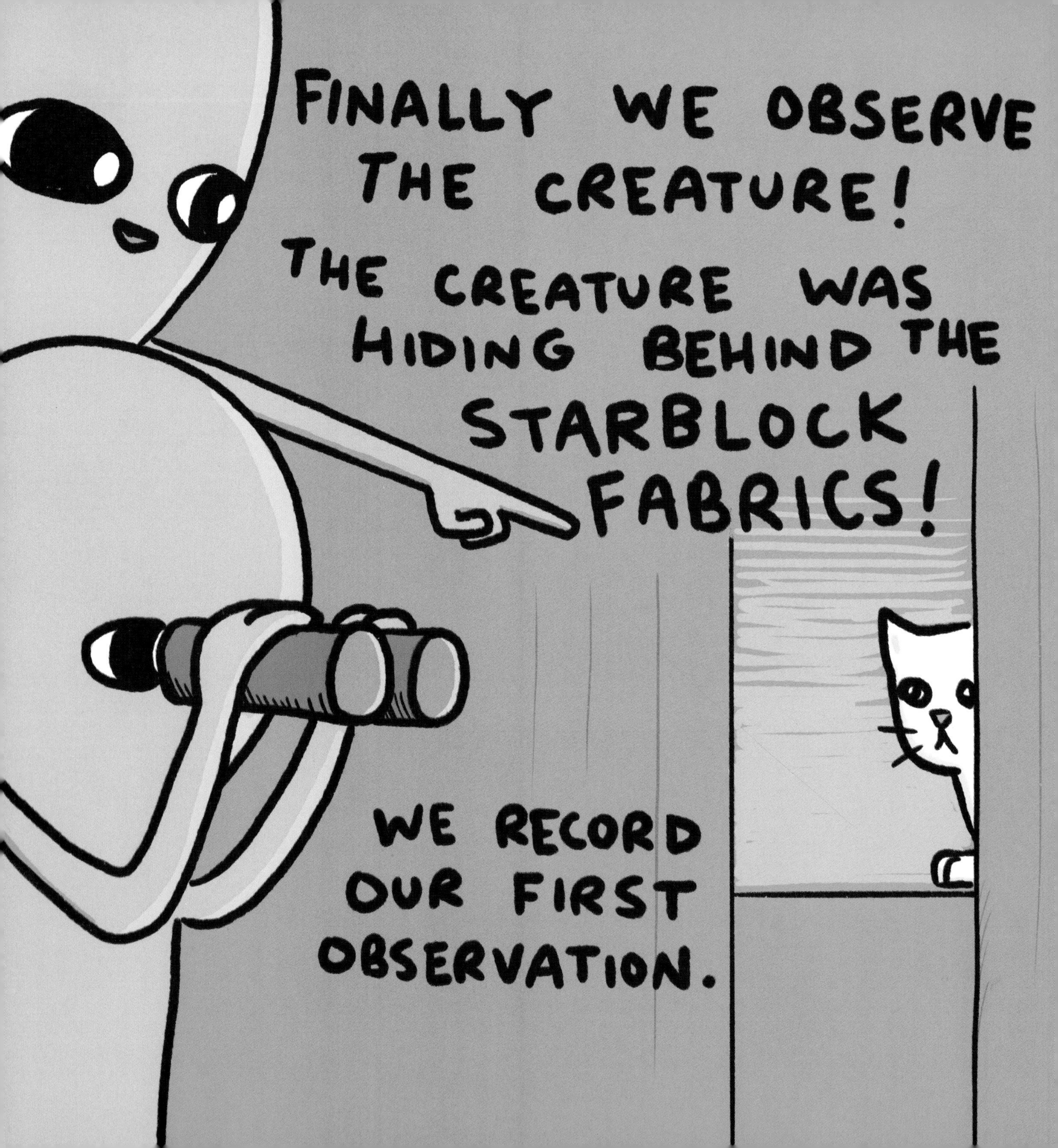
FINALLY WE OBSERVE THE CREATURE!
THE CREATURE WAS HIDING BEHIND THE STARBLOCK FABRICS!
WE RECORD OUR FIRST OBSERVATION.

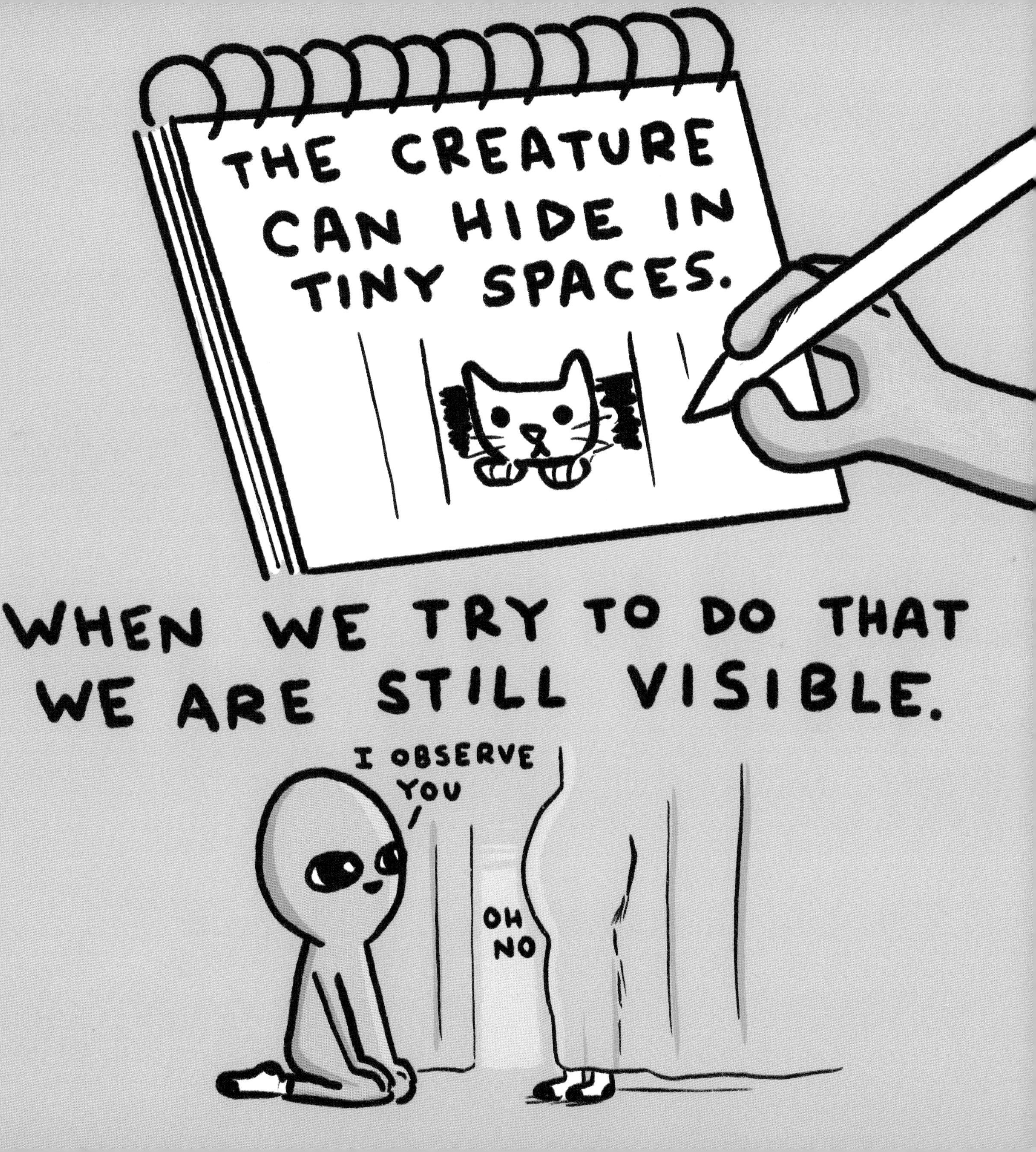
THE CREATURE CAN HIDE IN TINY SPACES.
WHEN WE TRY TO DO THAT WE ARE STILL VISIBLE.
I OBSERVE YOU
OH NO

SUDDENLY THE CREATURE JUMPS DOWN AND LANDS SOFTLY ON THE FOOT FABRIC.

THEN IT SNEAKS ACROSS THE FLOOR WITHOUT MAKING A SOUND!

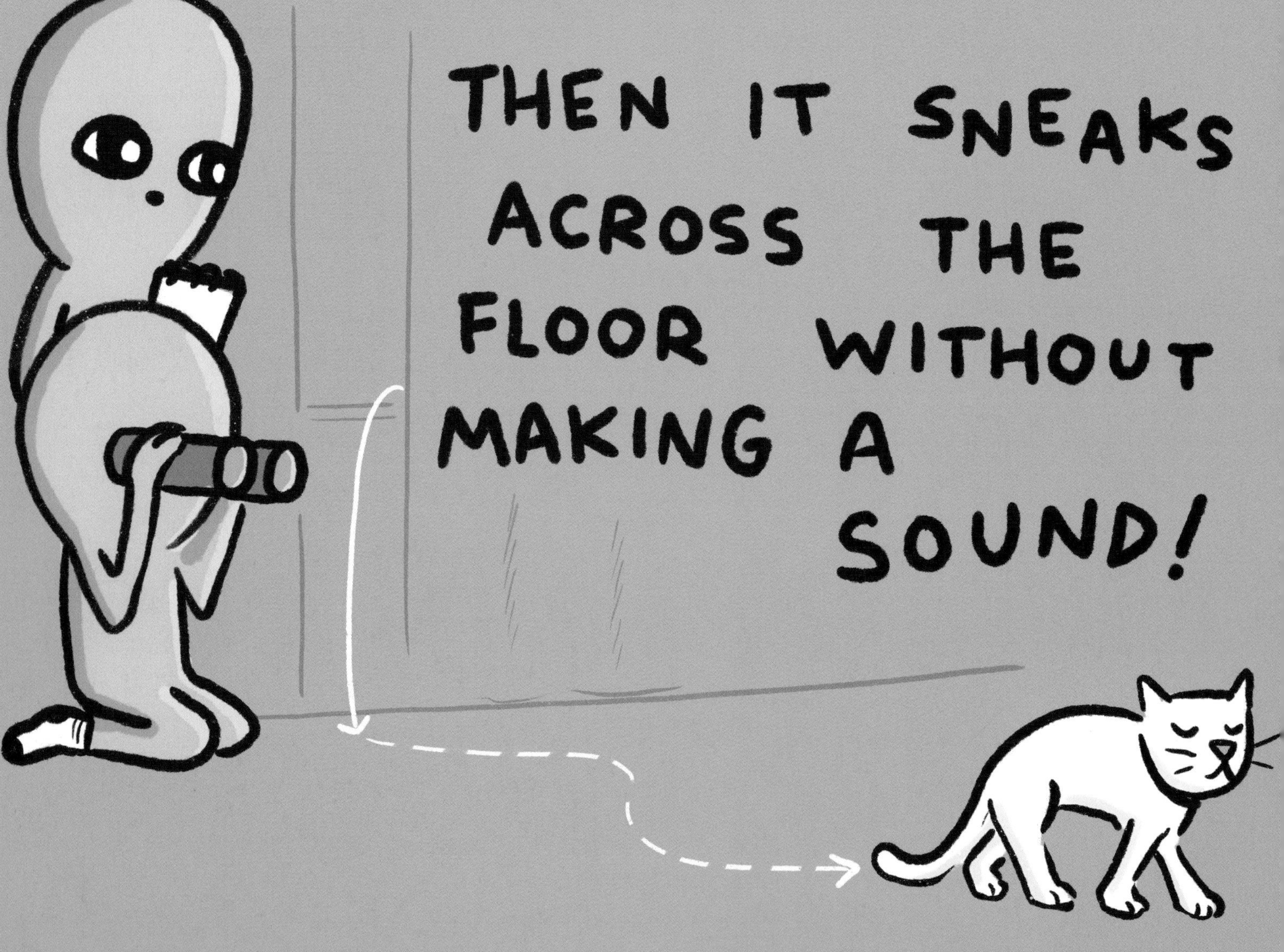

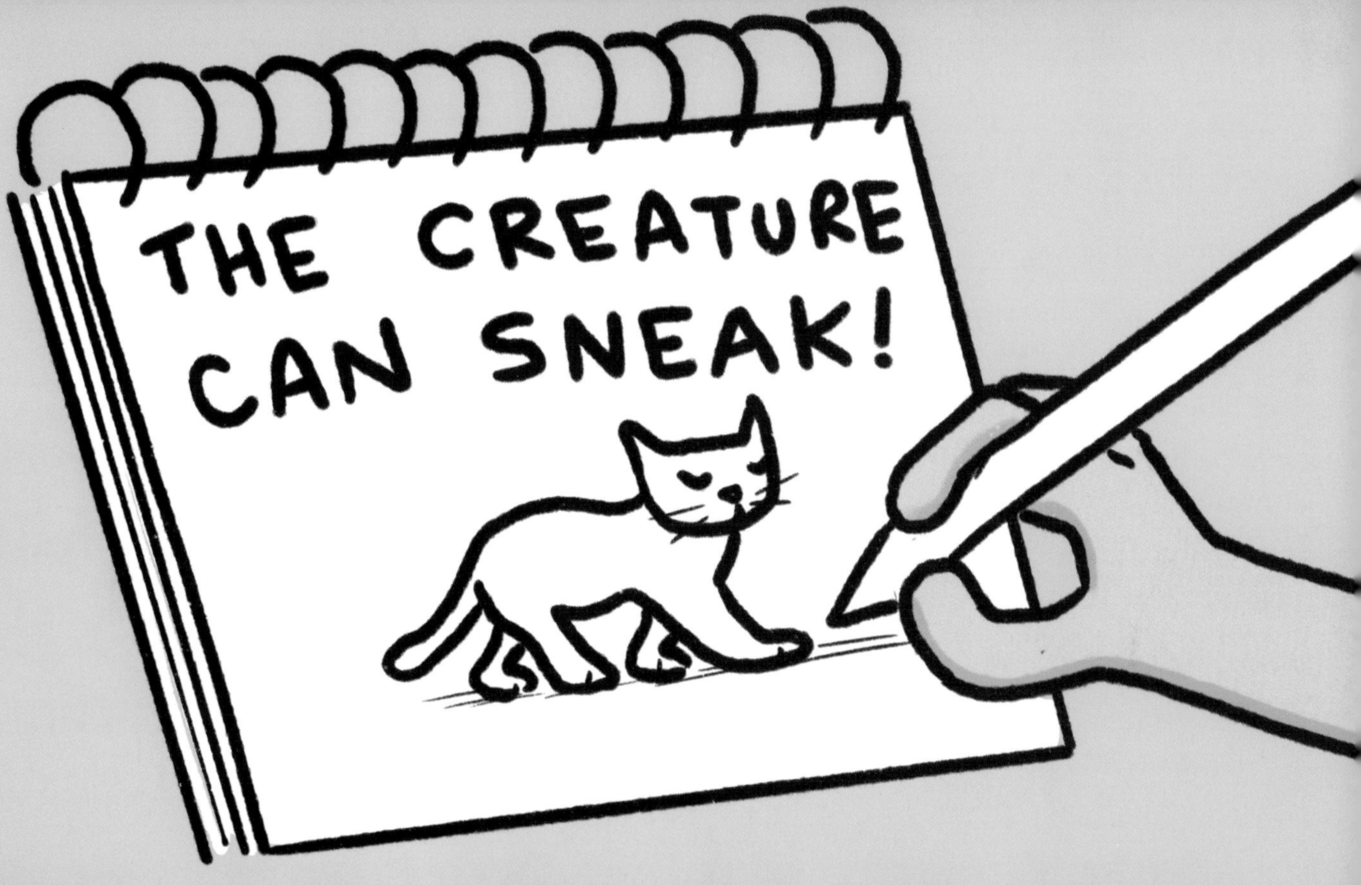
THE CREATURE CAN SNEAK!

WHEN WE TRY TO DO THAT WE ARE QUITE NOISY.

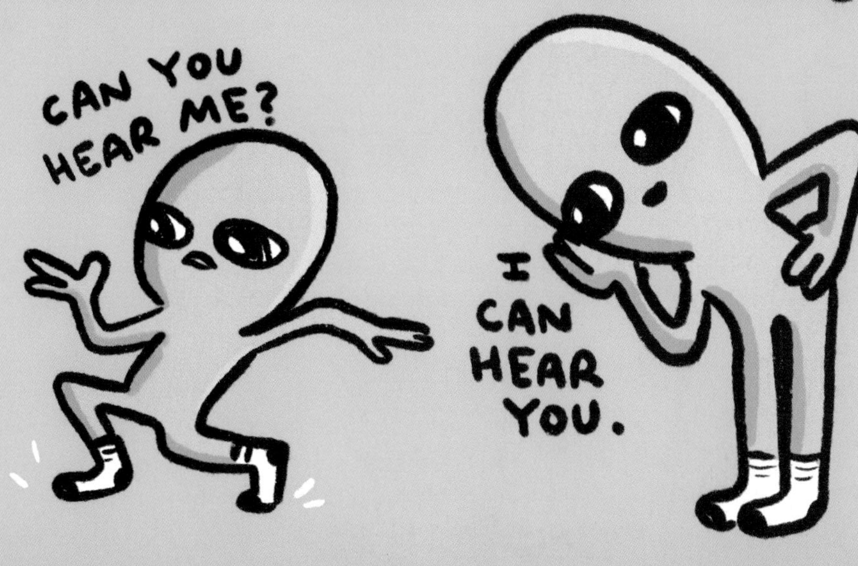
CAN YOU HEAR ME?
I CAN HEAR YOU.

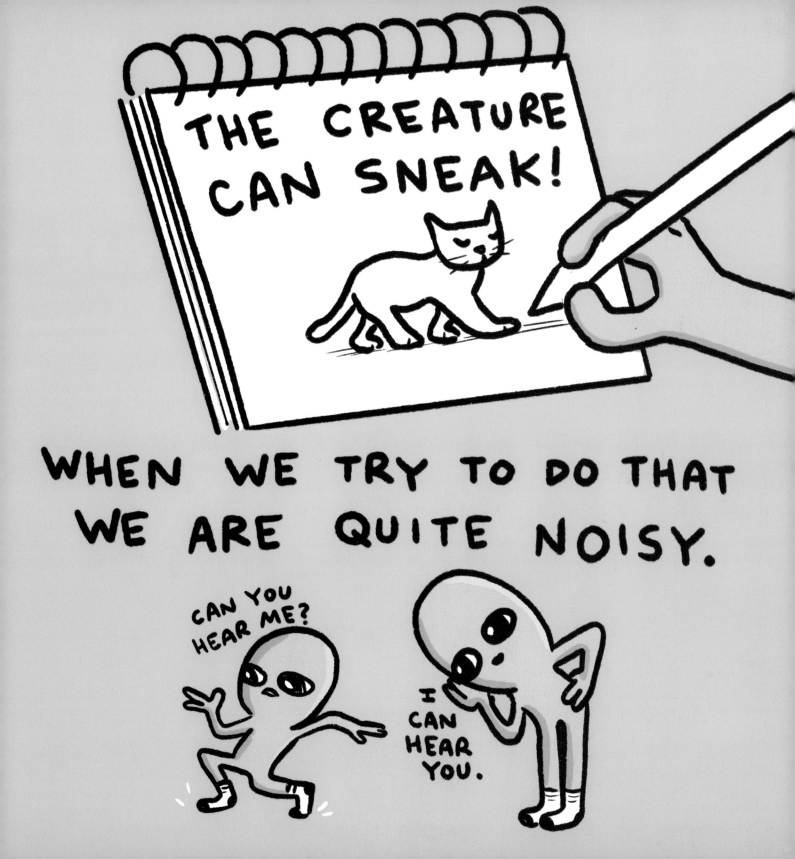

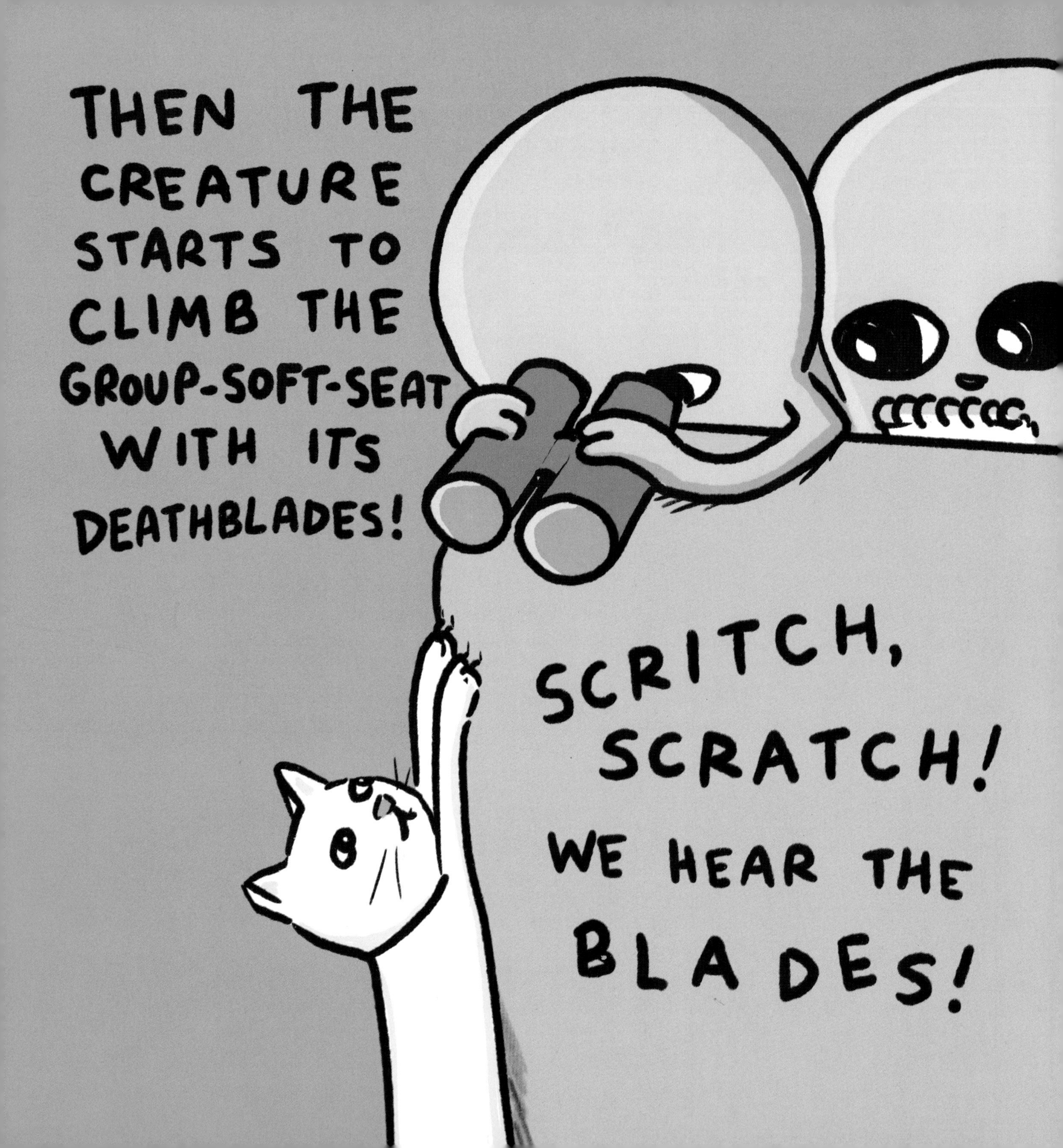
THEN THE CREATURE STARTS TO CLIMB THE GROUP-SOFT-SEAT WITH ITS DEATHBLADES!
SCRITCH, SCRATCH!
WE HEAR THE BLADES!

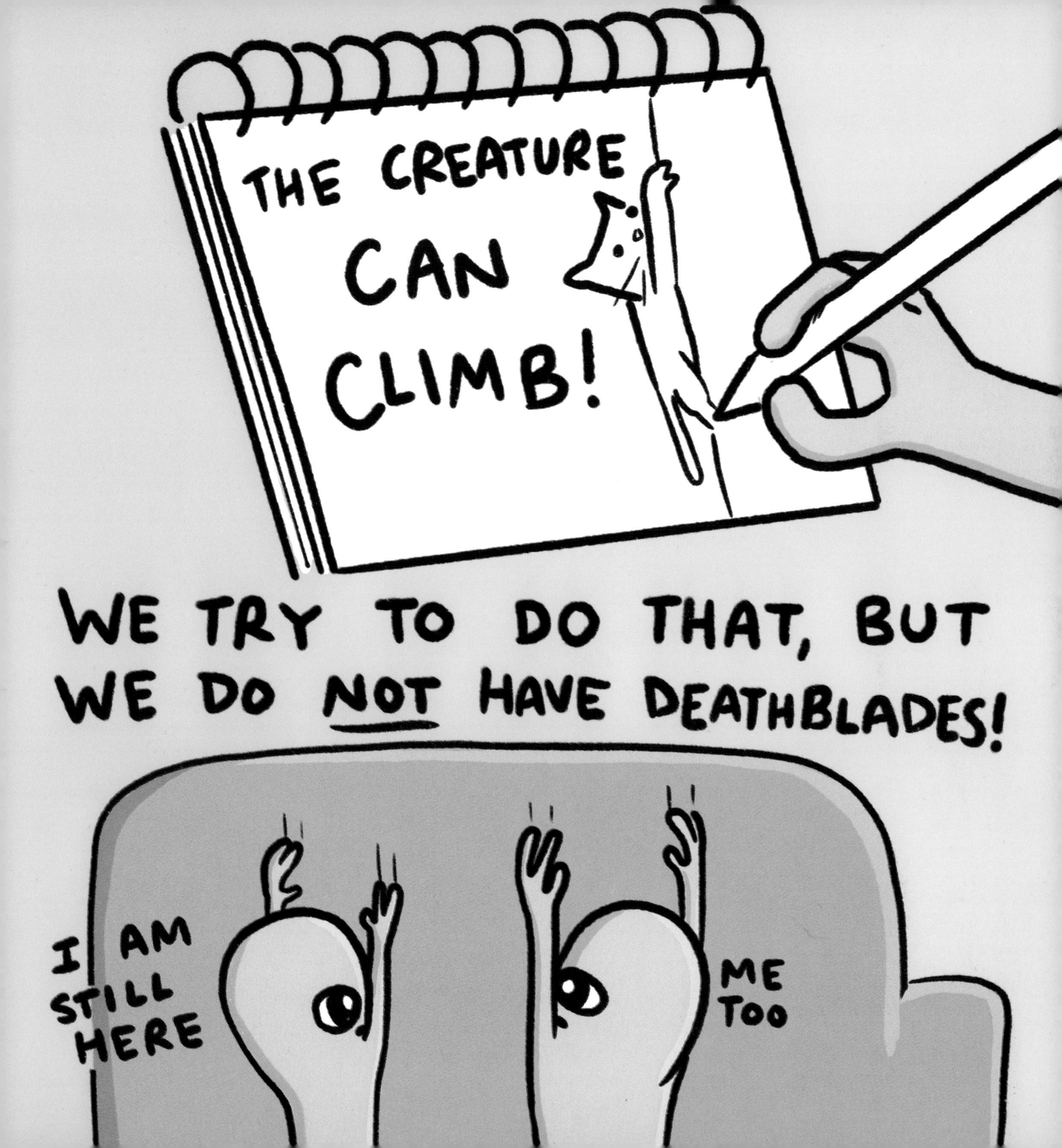
THE CREATURE CAN CLIMB!
WE TRY TO DO THAT, BUT WE DO NOT HAVE DEATHBLADES!
I AM STILL HERE
ME TOO

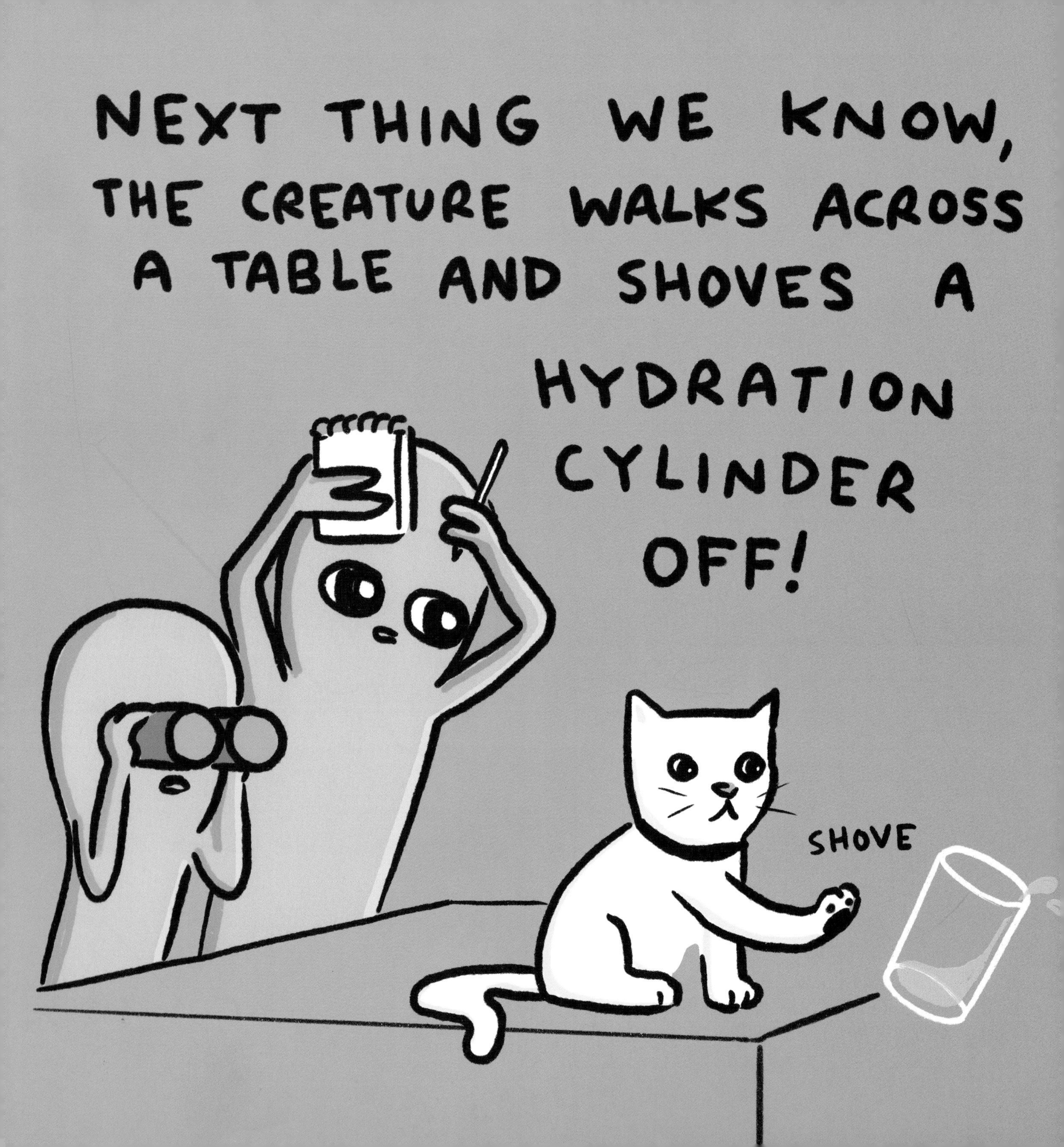
NEXT THING WE KNOW, THE CREATURE WALKS ACROSS A TABLE AND SHOVES A HYDRATION CYLINDER OFF!
SHOVE

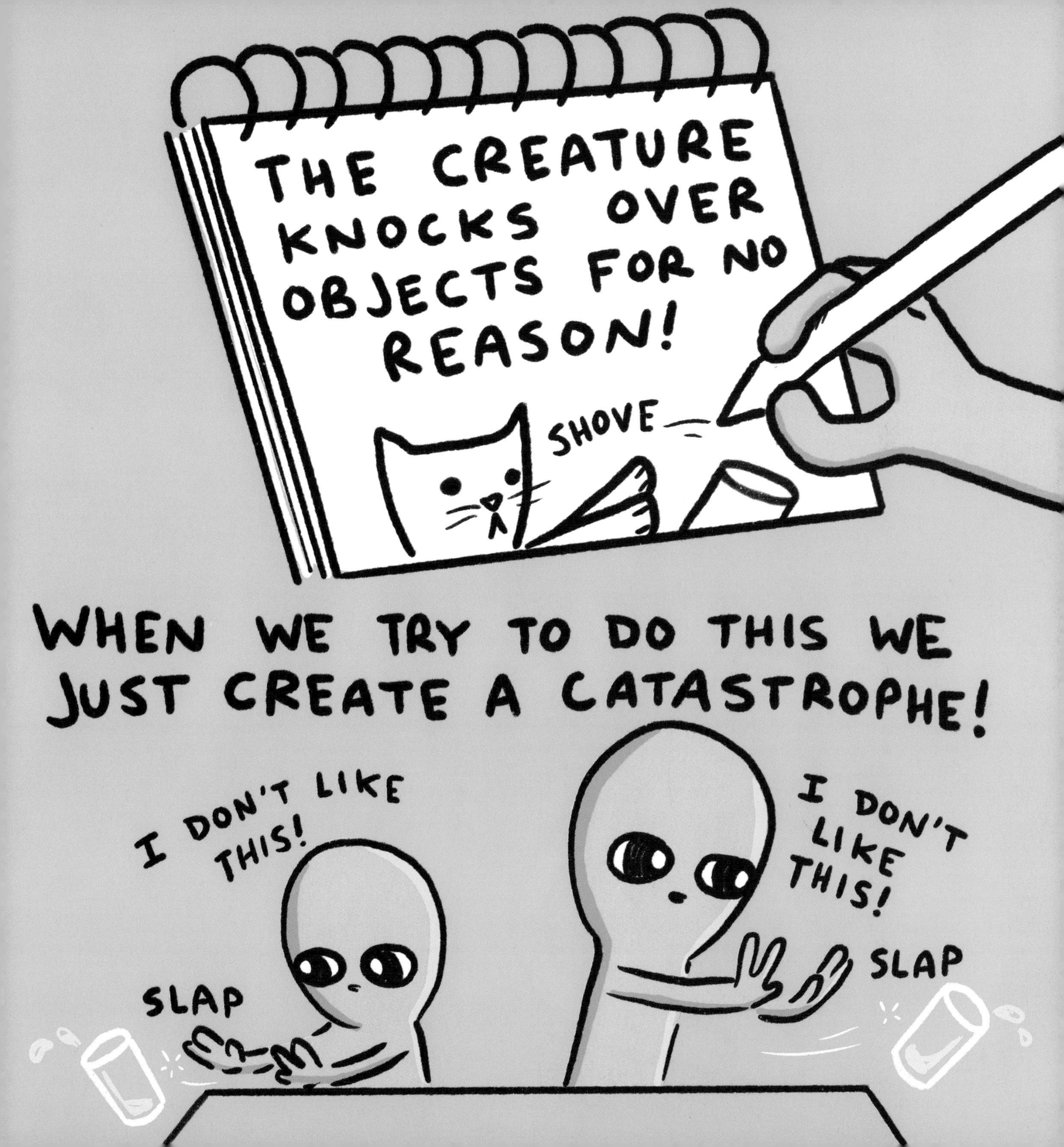
THE CREATURE KNOCKS OVER OBJECTS FOR NO REASON!
SHOVE
WHEN WE TRY TO DO THIS WE JUST CREATE A CATASTROPHE!
I DON'T LIKE THIS!
SLAP
I DON'T LIKE THIS!
SLAP

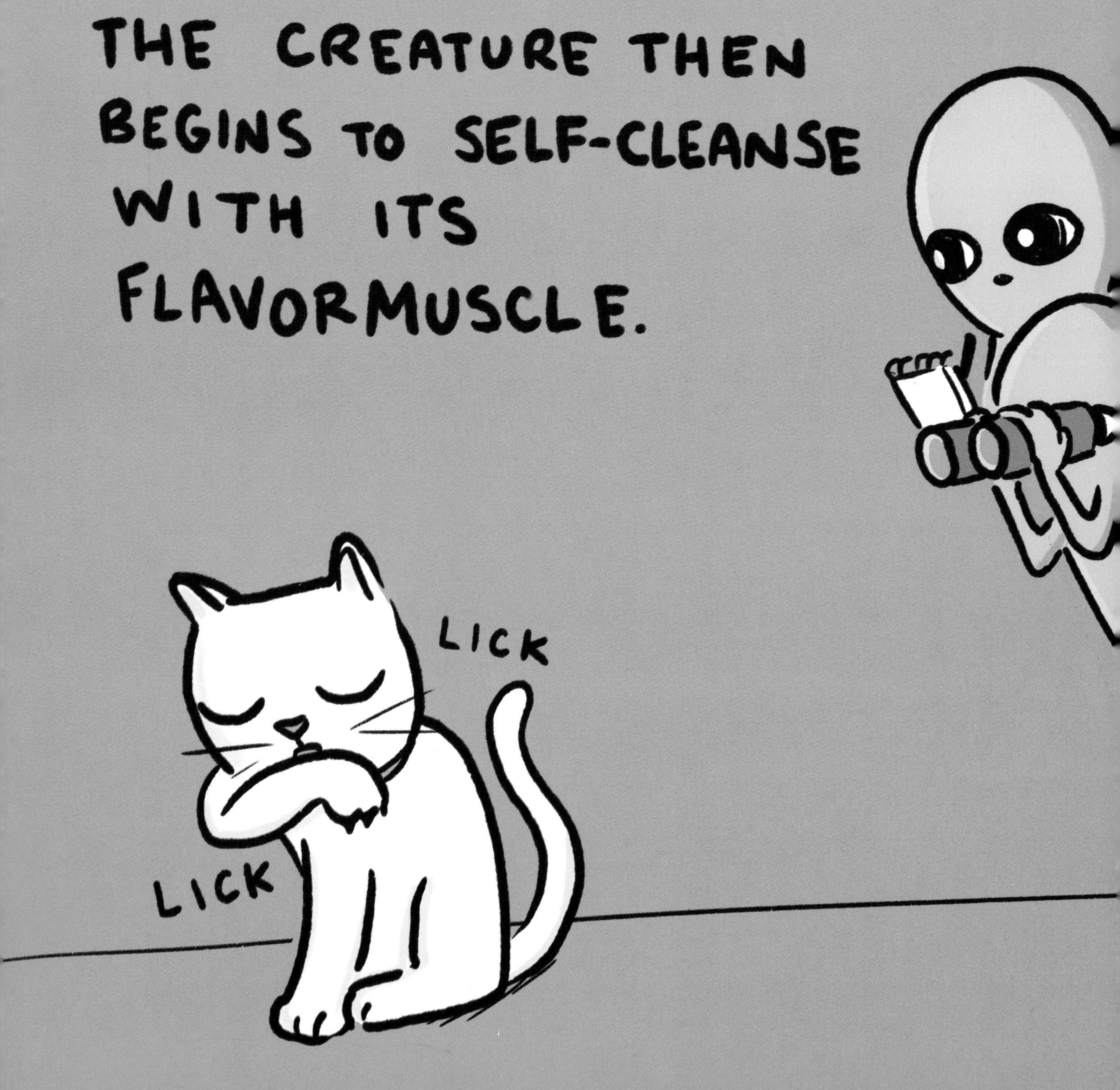
THE CREATURE THEN BEGINS TO SELF-CLEANSE WITH ITS FLAVORMUSCLE.
LICK
LICK

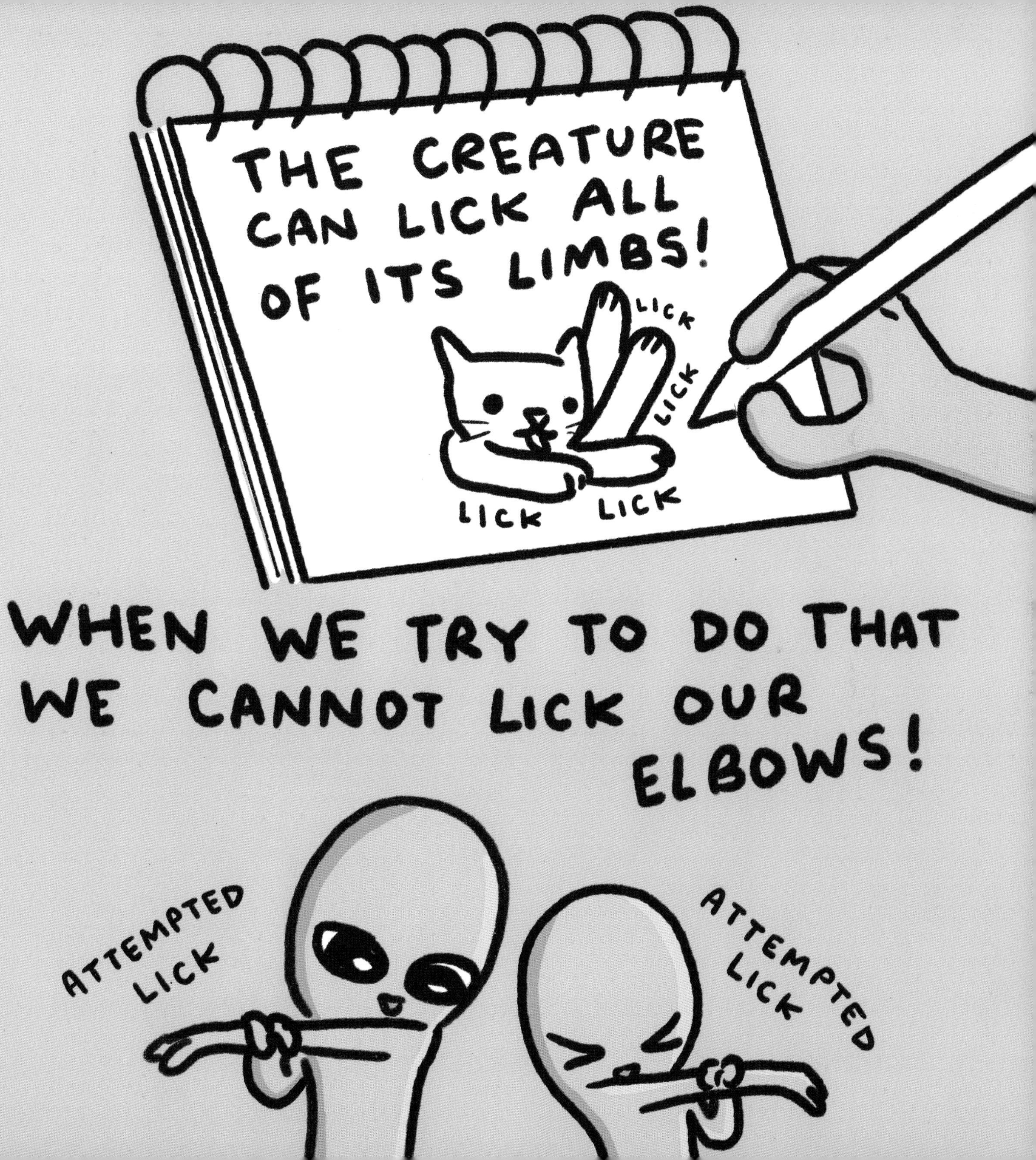
THE CREATURE CAN LICK ALL OF ITS LIMBS!
LICK
LICK
LICK
LICK
LICK
WHEN WE TRY TO DO THAT WE CANNOT LICK OUR ELBOWS!
ATTEMPTED LICK
ATTEMPTED LICK

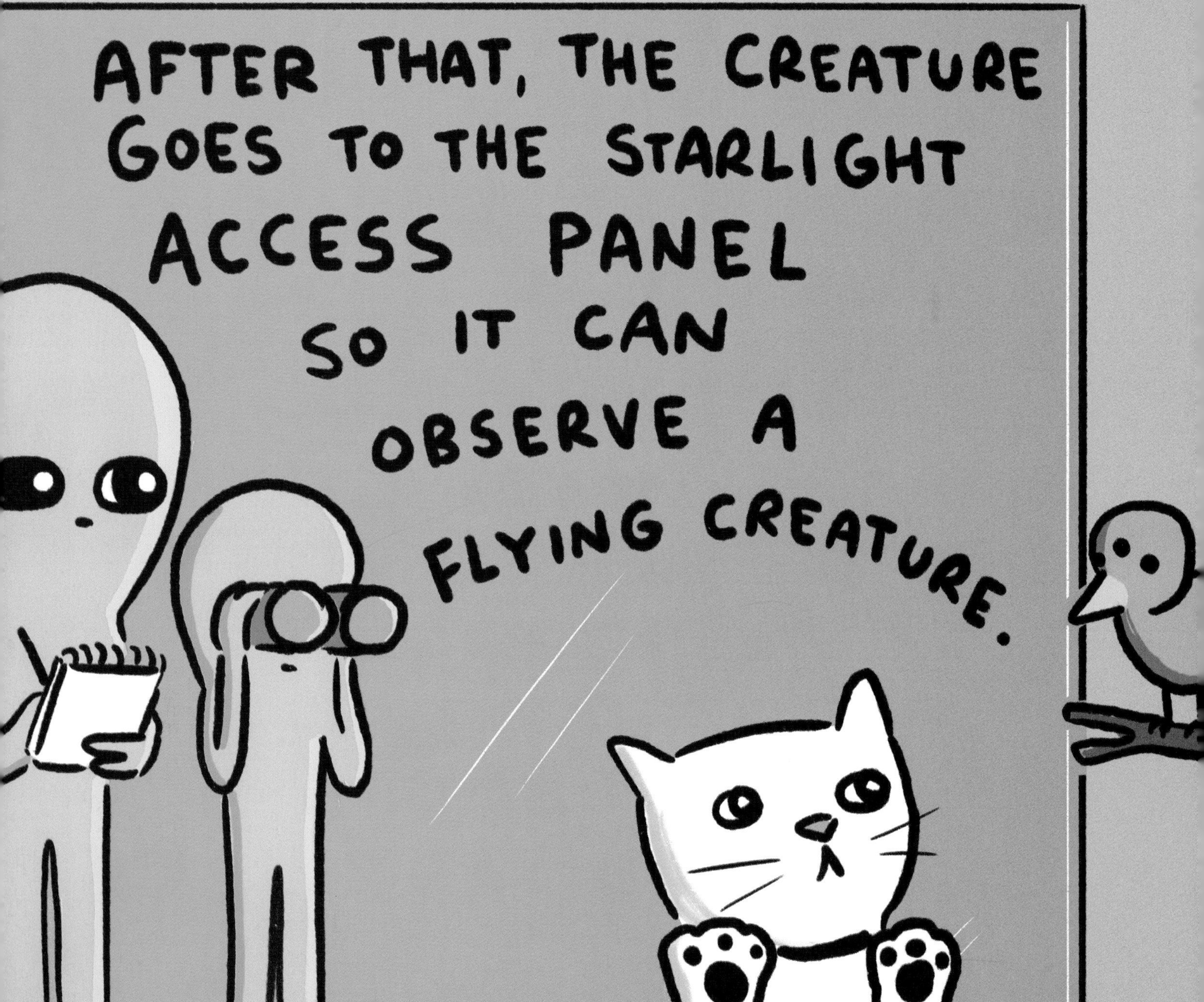
AFTER THAT, THE CREATURE GOES TO THE STARLIGHT ACCESS PANEL SO IT CAN OBSERVE A FLYING CREATURE.

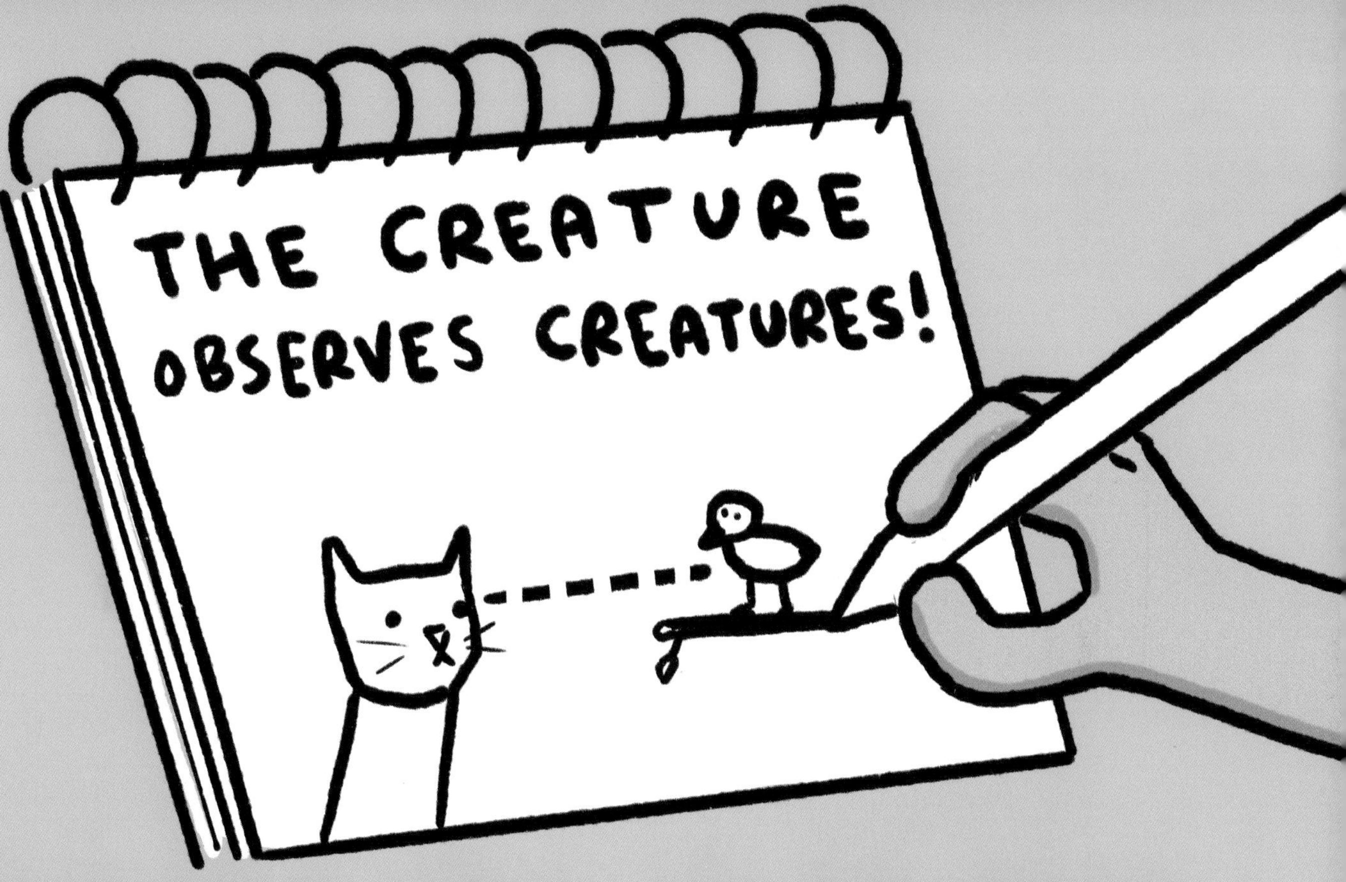
THE CREATURE
OBSERVES CREATURES!

WHEN WE TRY TO DO THAT...
WAIT- WE ARE DOING THAT!

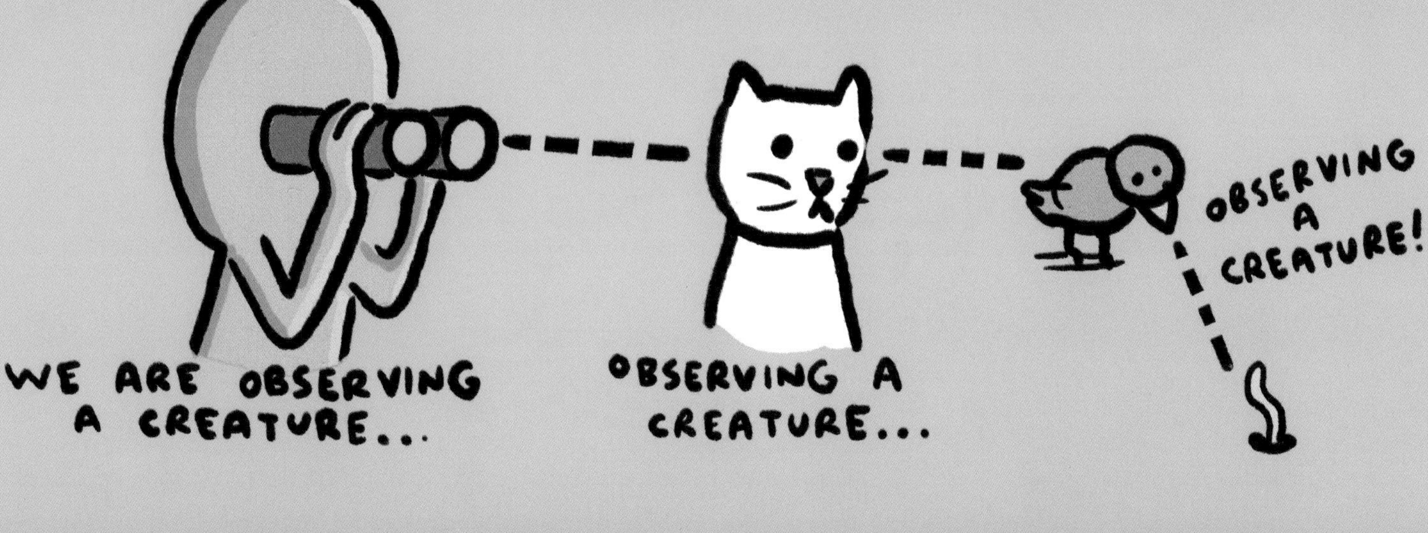
WE ARE OBSERVING
A CREATURE...
OBSERVING A
CREATURE...
OBSERVING
A
CREATURE!

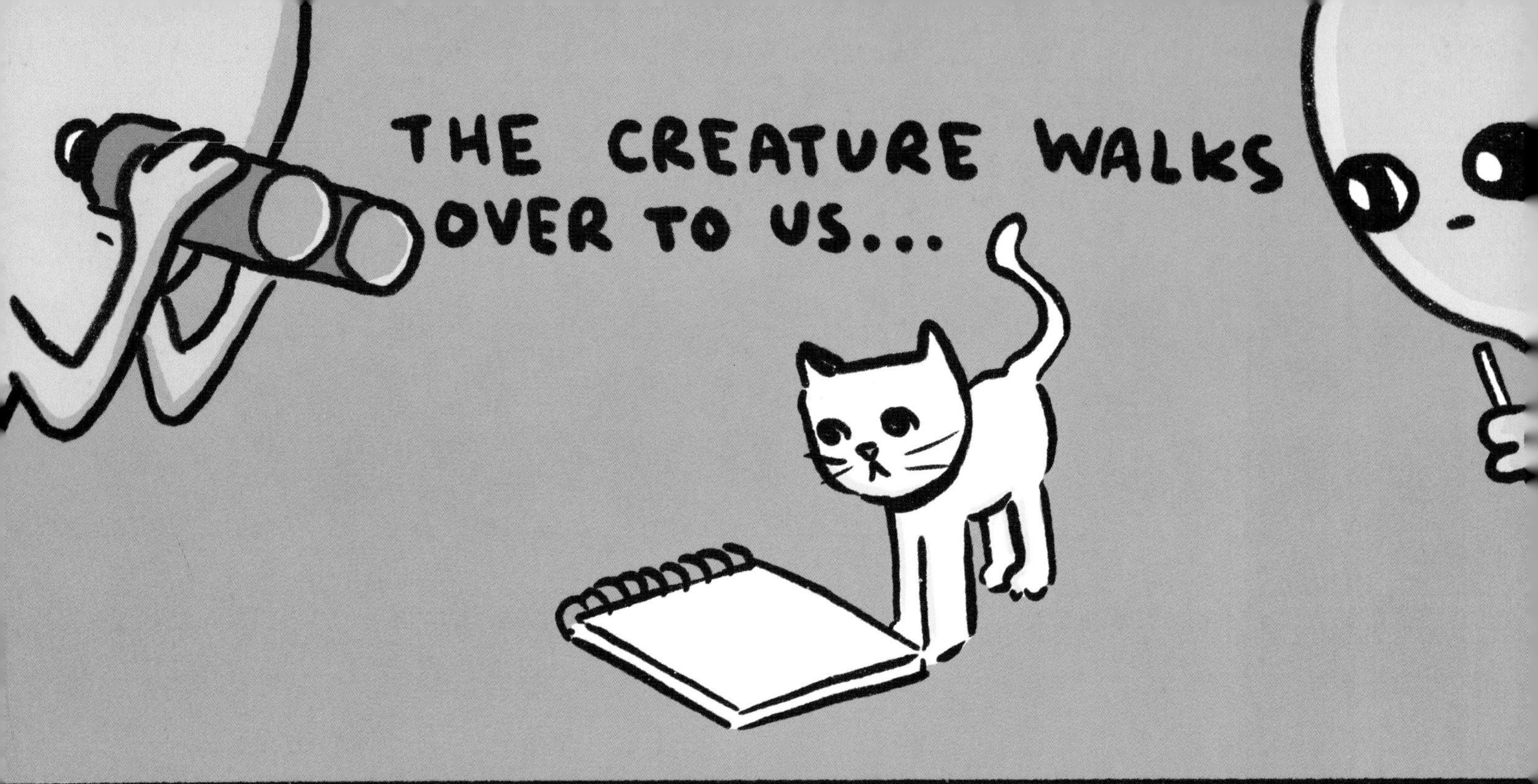
THE CREATURE WALKS OVER TO US...

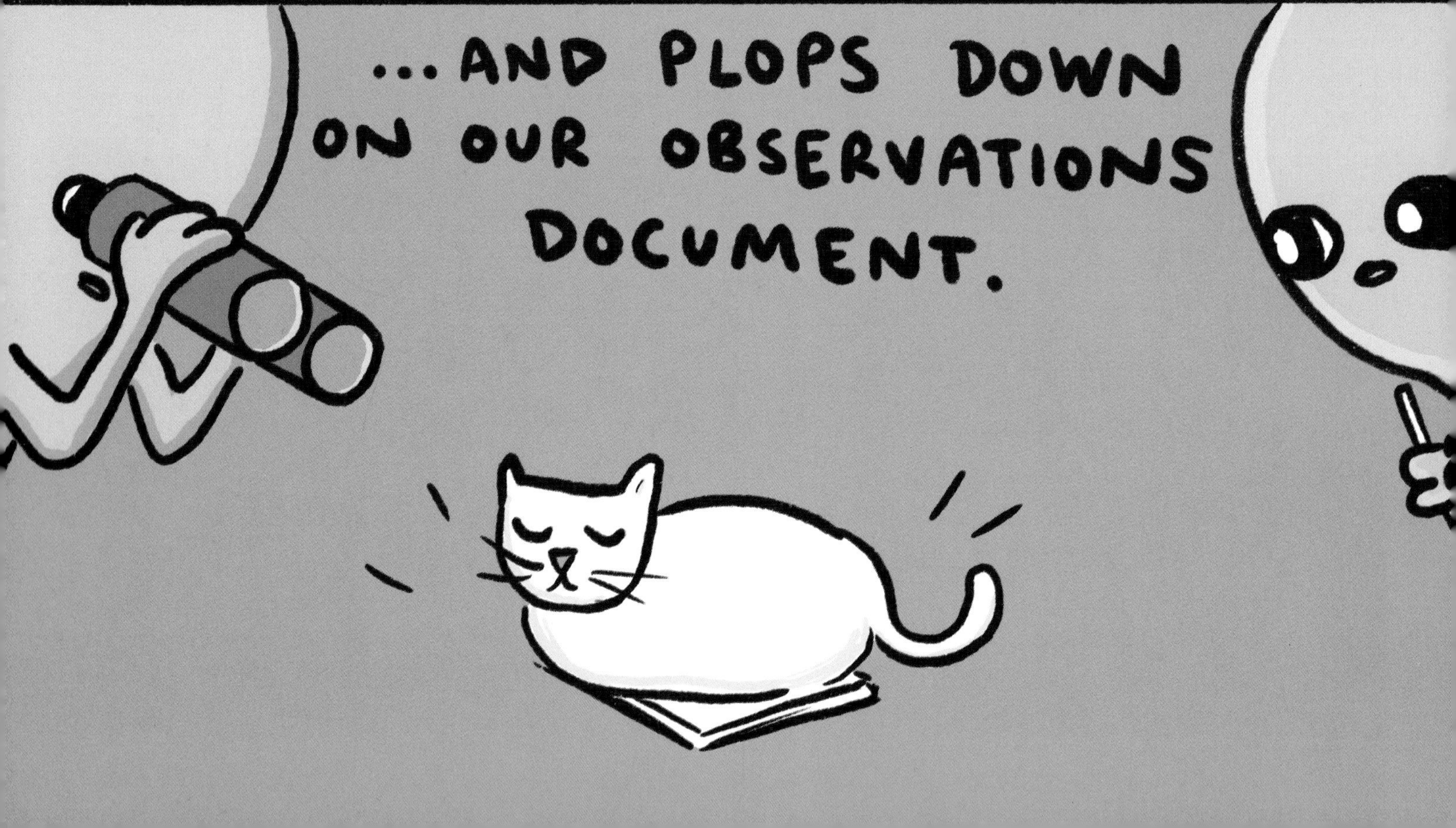
...AND PLOPS DOWN ON OUR OBSERVATIONS DOCUMENT.

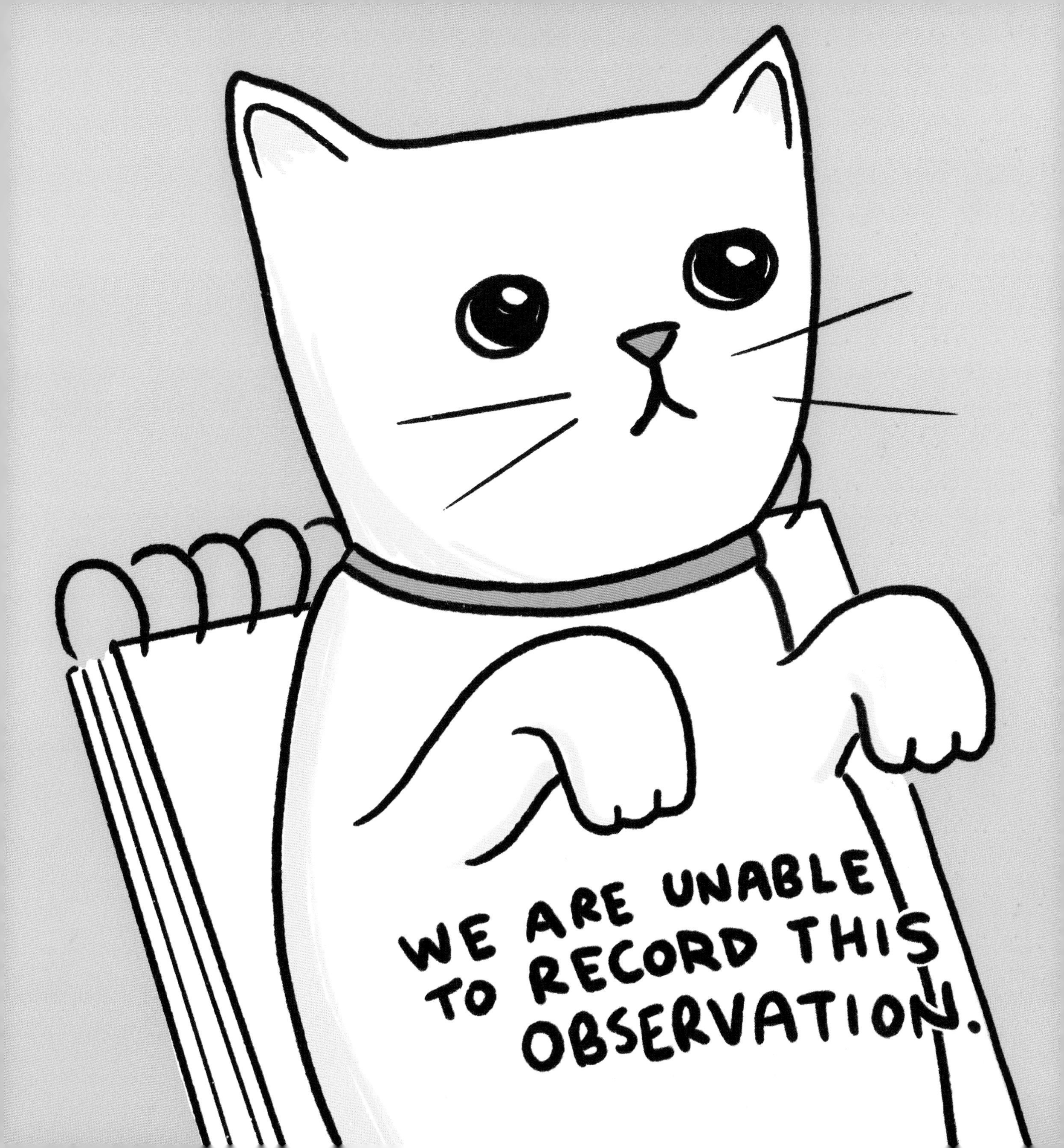
WE ARE UNABLE
TO RECORD THIS
OBSERVATION.

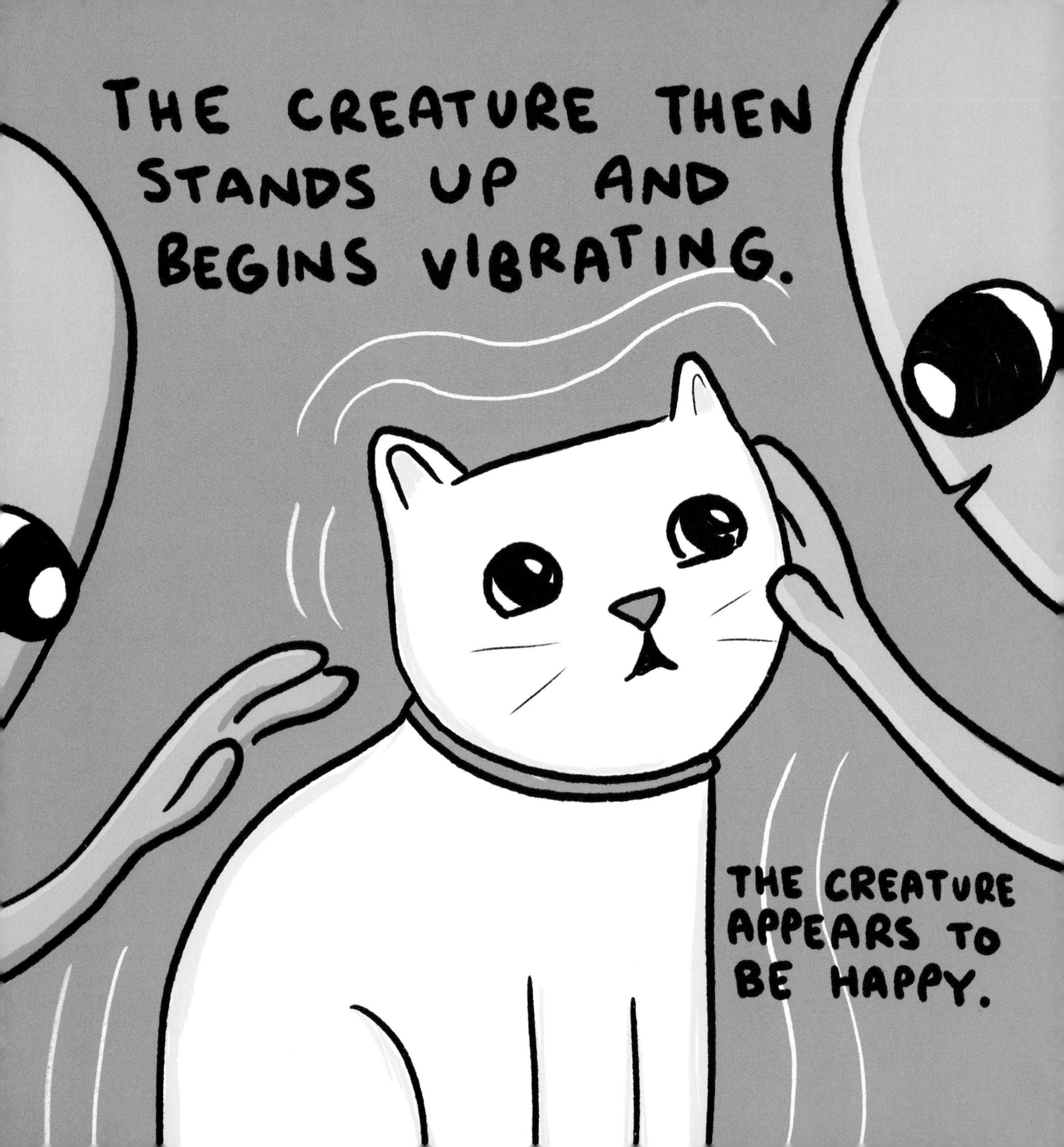
THE CREATURE THEN STANDS UP AND BEGINS VIBRATING.
THE CREATURE APPEARS TO BE HAPPY.

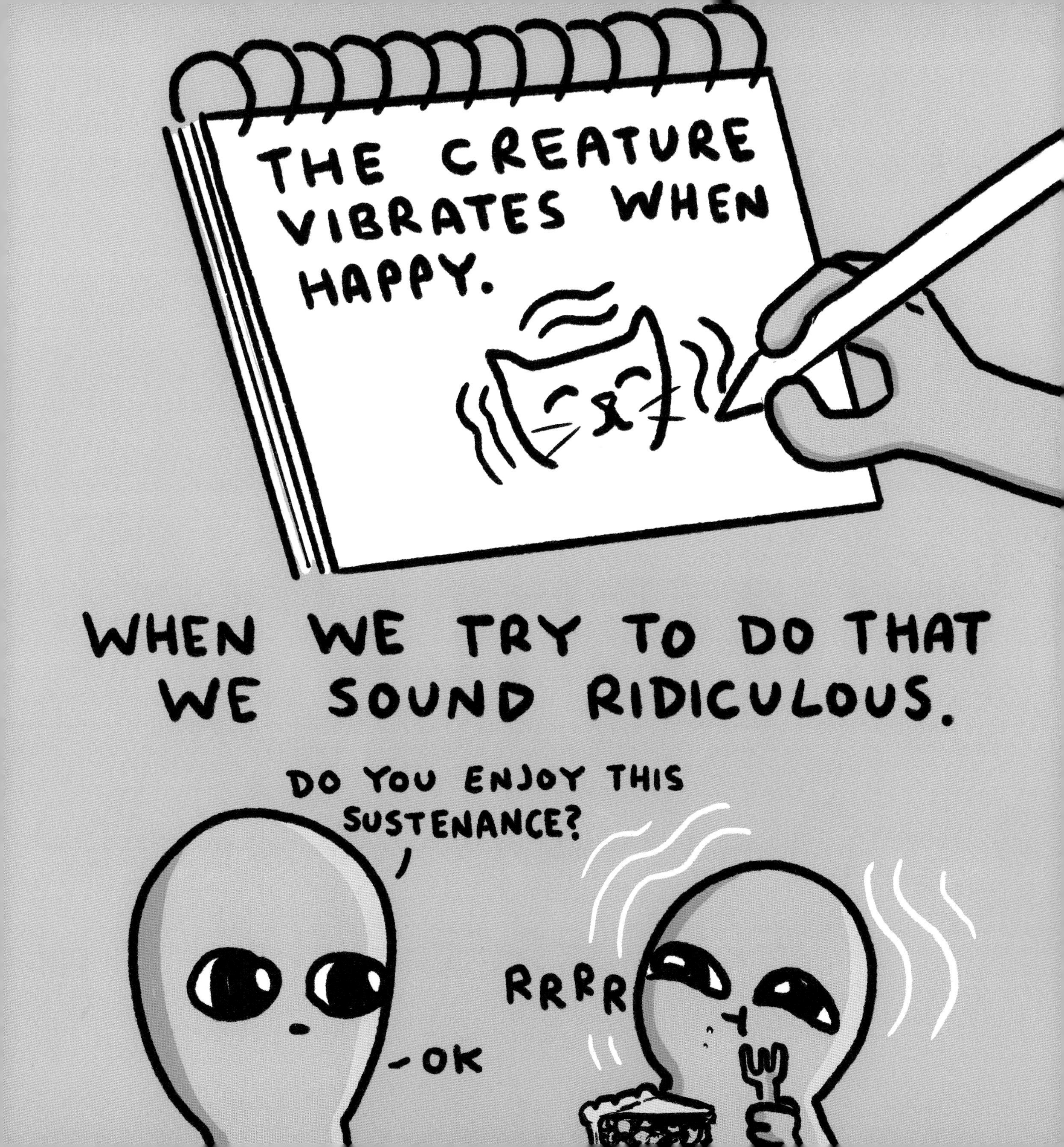
THE CREATURE VIBRATES WHEN HAPPY.
WHEN WE TRY TO DO THAT WE SOUND RIDICULOUS.
DO YOU ENJOY THIS SUSTENANCE?
RRRR
-OK

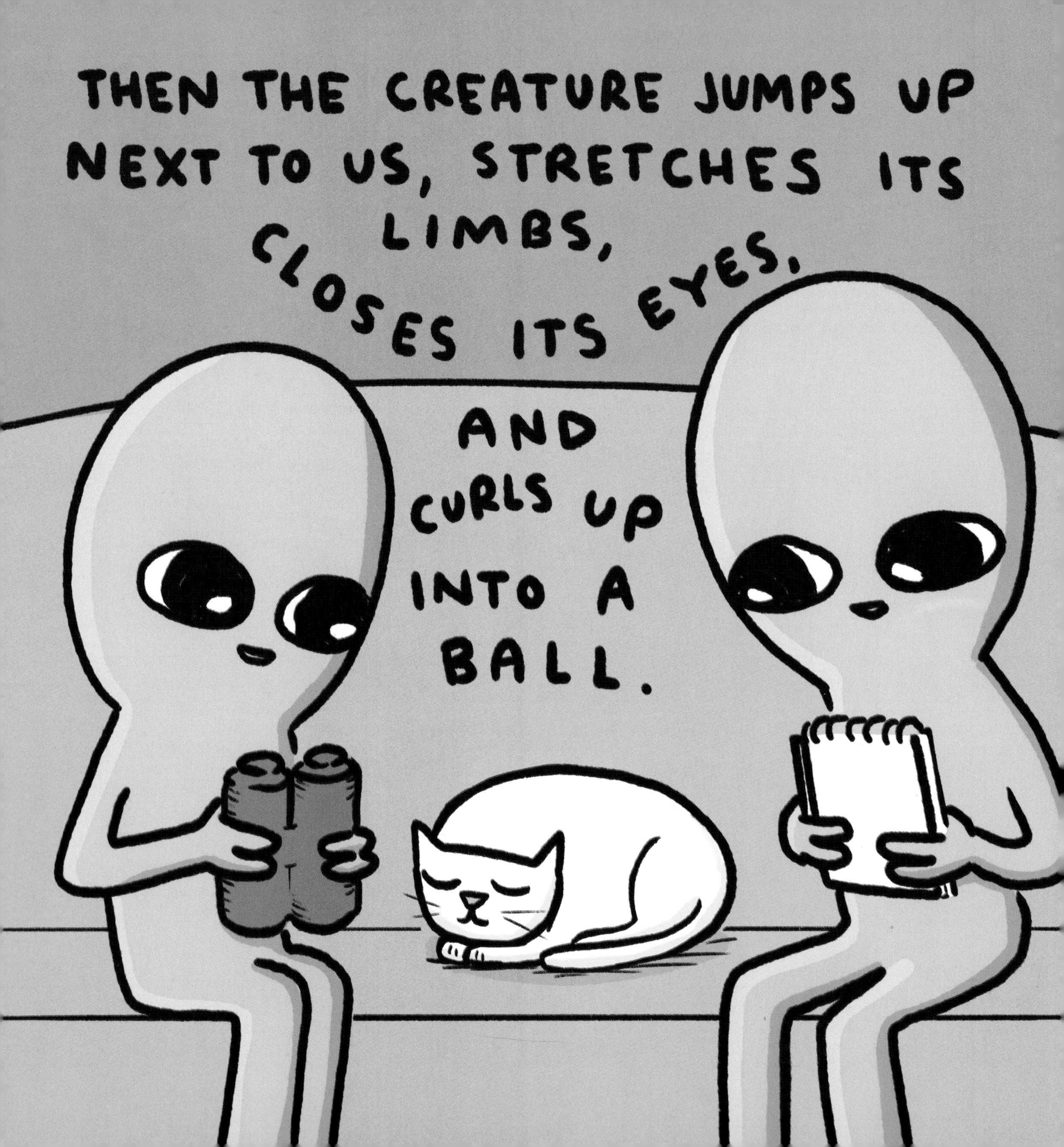
THEN THE CREATURE JUMPS UP NEXT TO US, STRETCHES ITS LIMBS,
CLOSES ITS EYES,
AND CURLS UP INTO A BALL.

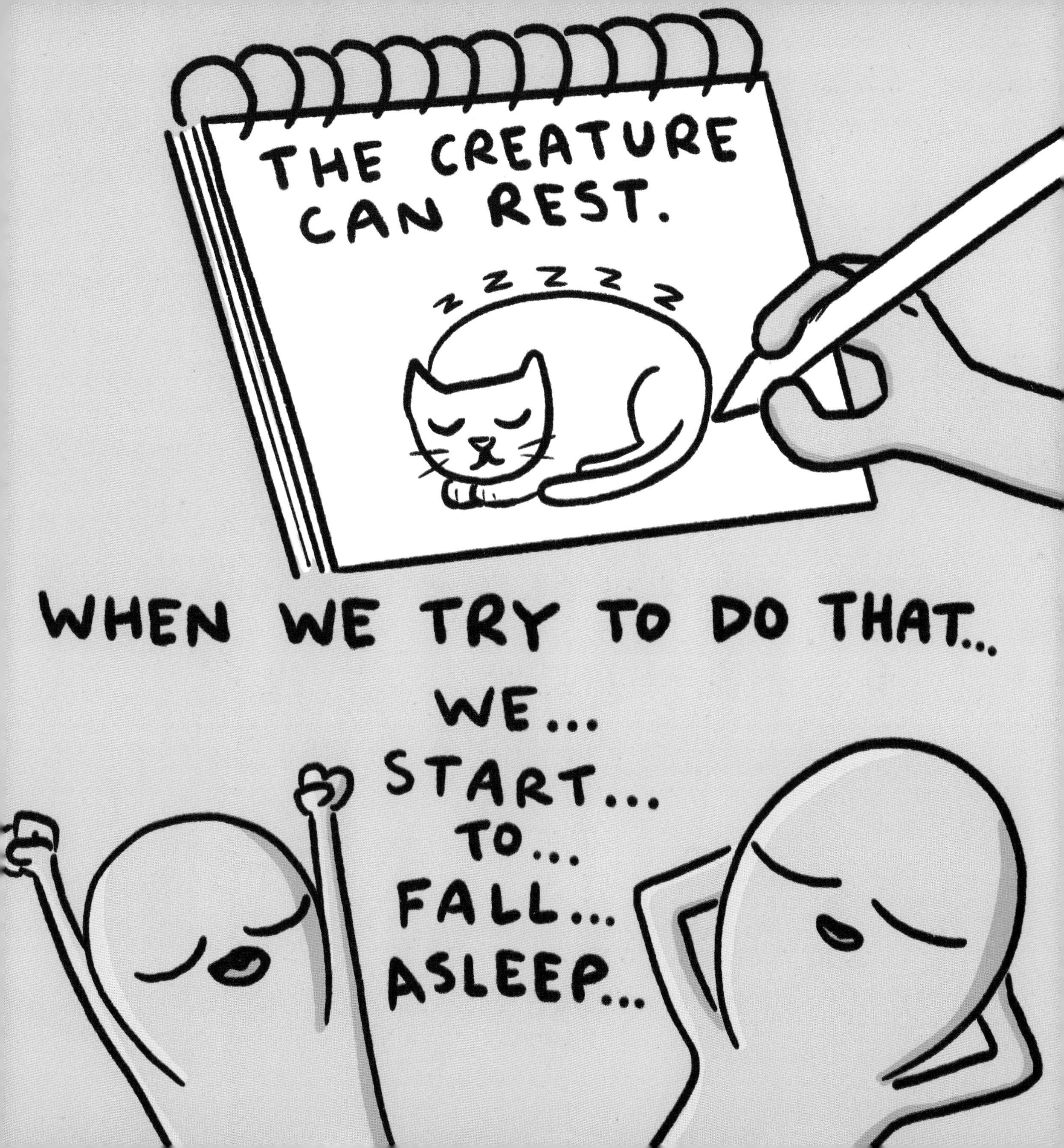
THE CREATURE CAN REST.
WHEN WE TRY TO DO THAT...
WE...
START...
TO...
FALL...
ASLEEP...

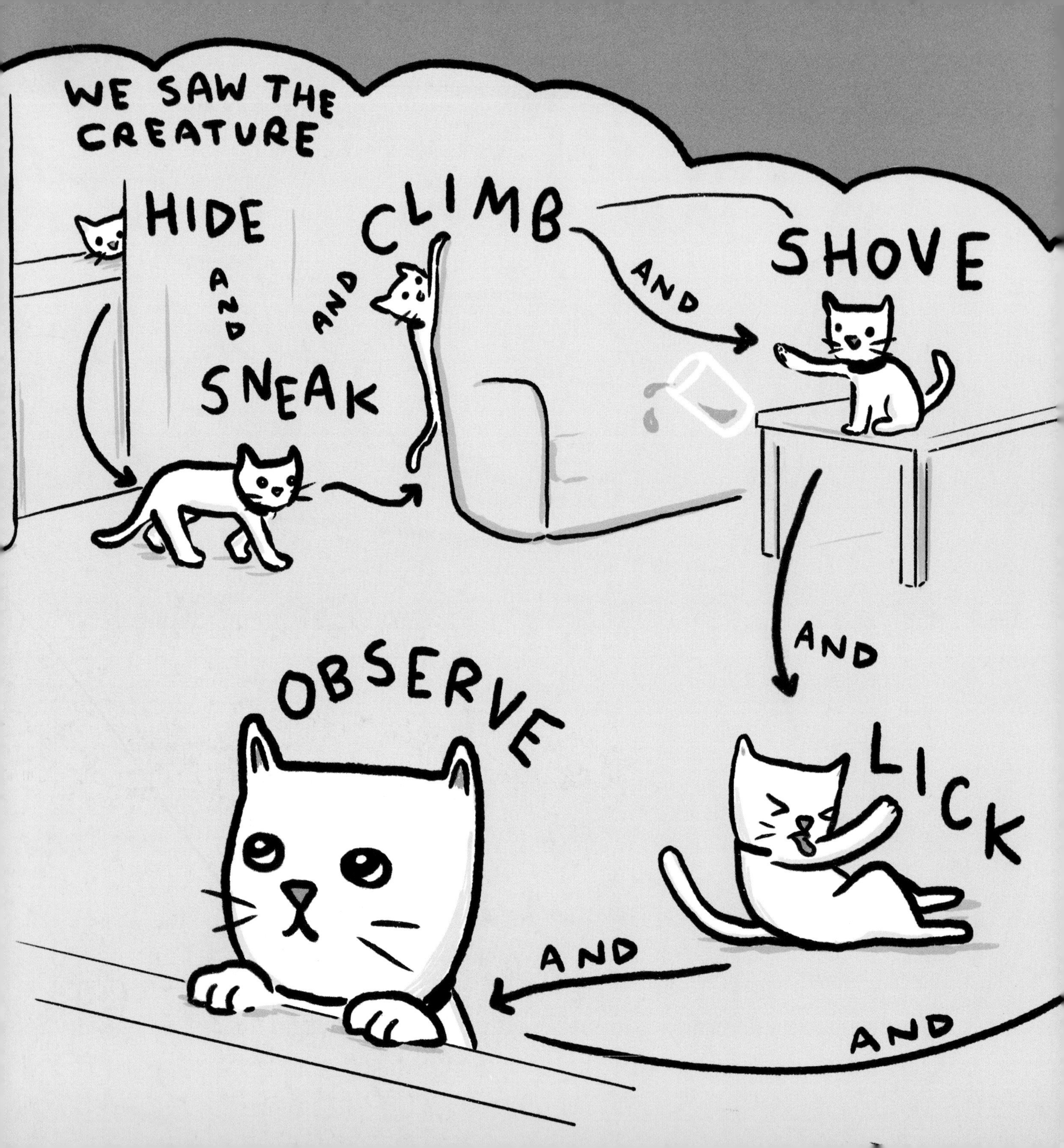
WE SAW THE CREATURE
HIDE
AND
SNEAK
AND
CLIMB
AND
SHOVE
AND
LICK
AND
OBSERVE
AND

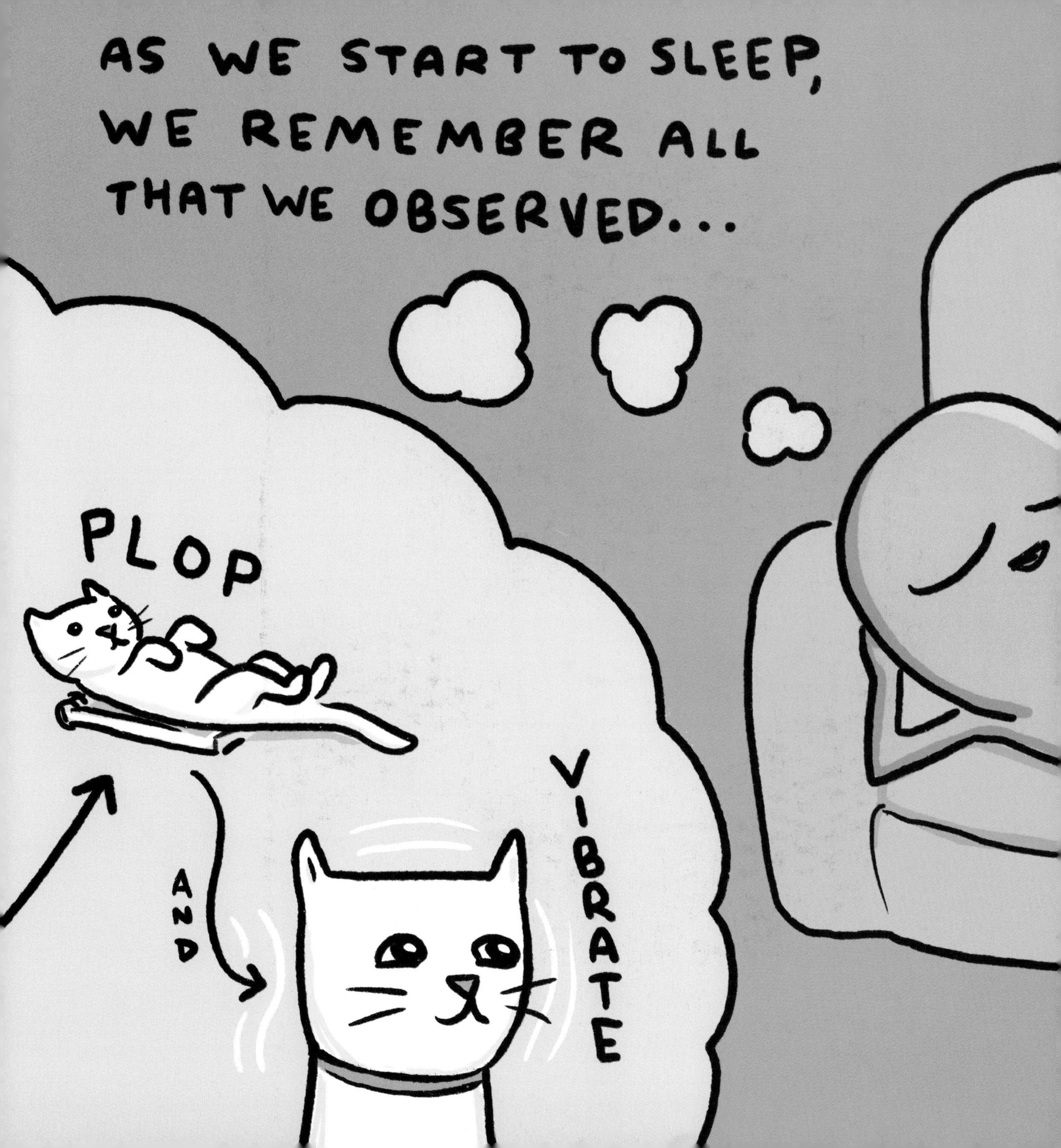
AS WE START TO SLEEP, WE REMEMBER ALL THAT WE OBSERVED...
PLOP
AND
VIBRATE

AND THEN THE CREATURE TAKES A CREATURE NAP.

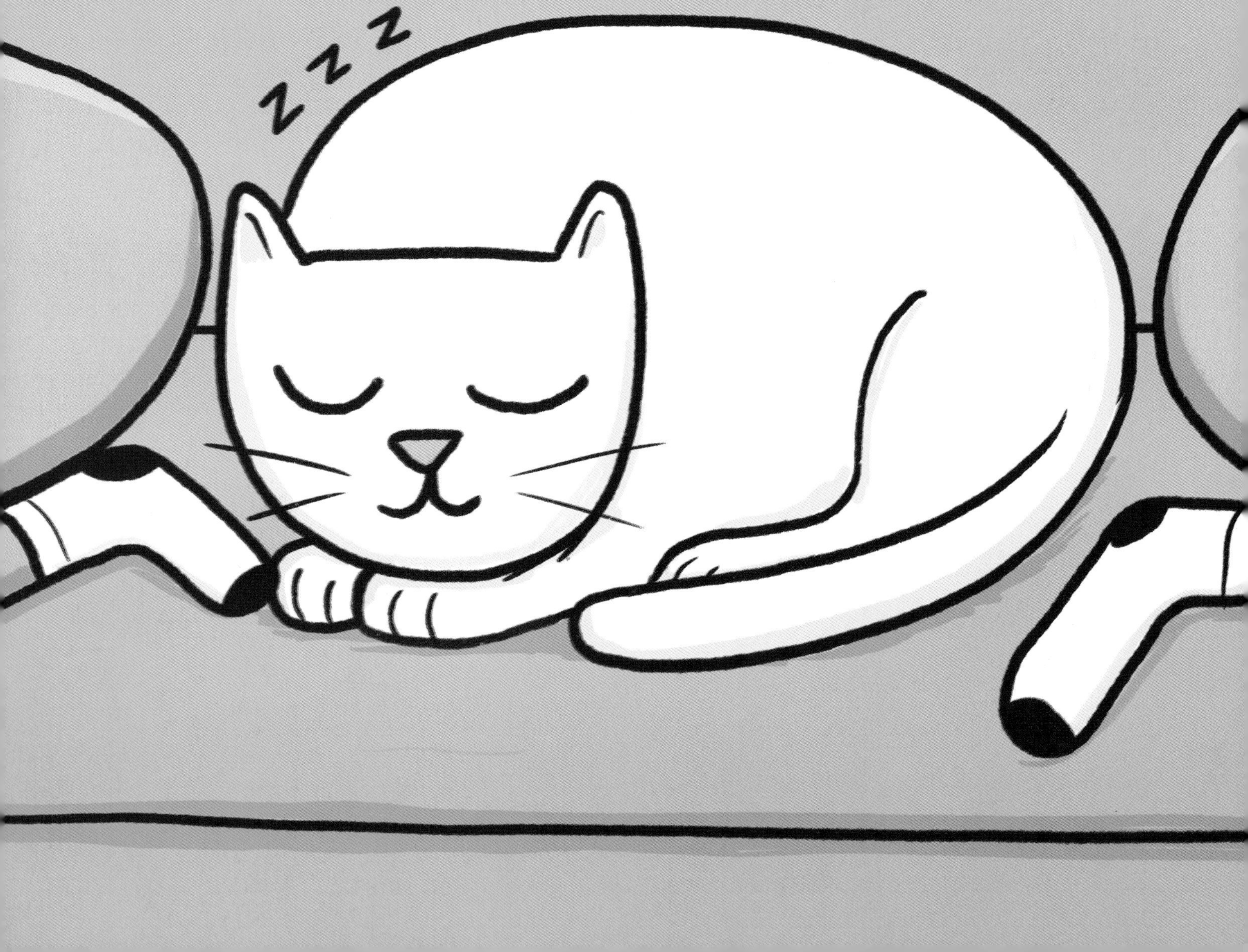
ZZZ

AND WE TAKE A CREATURE NAP TOO.

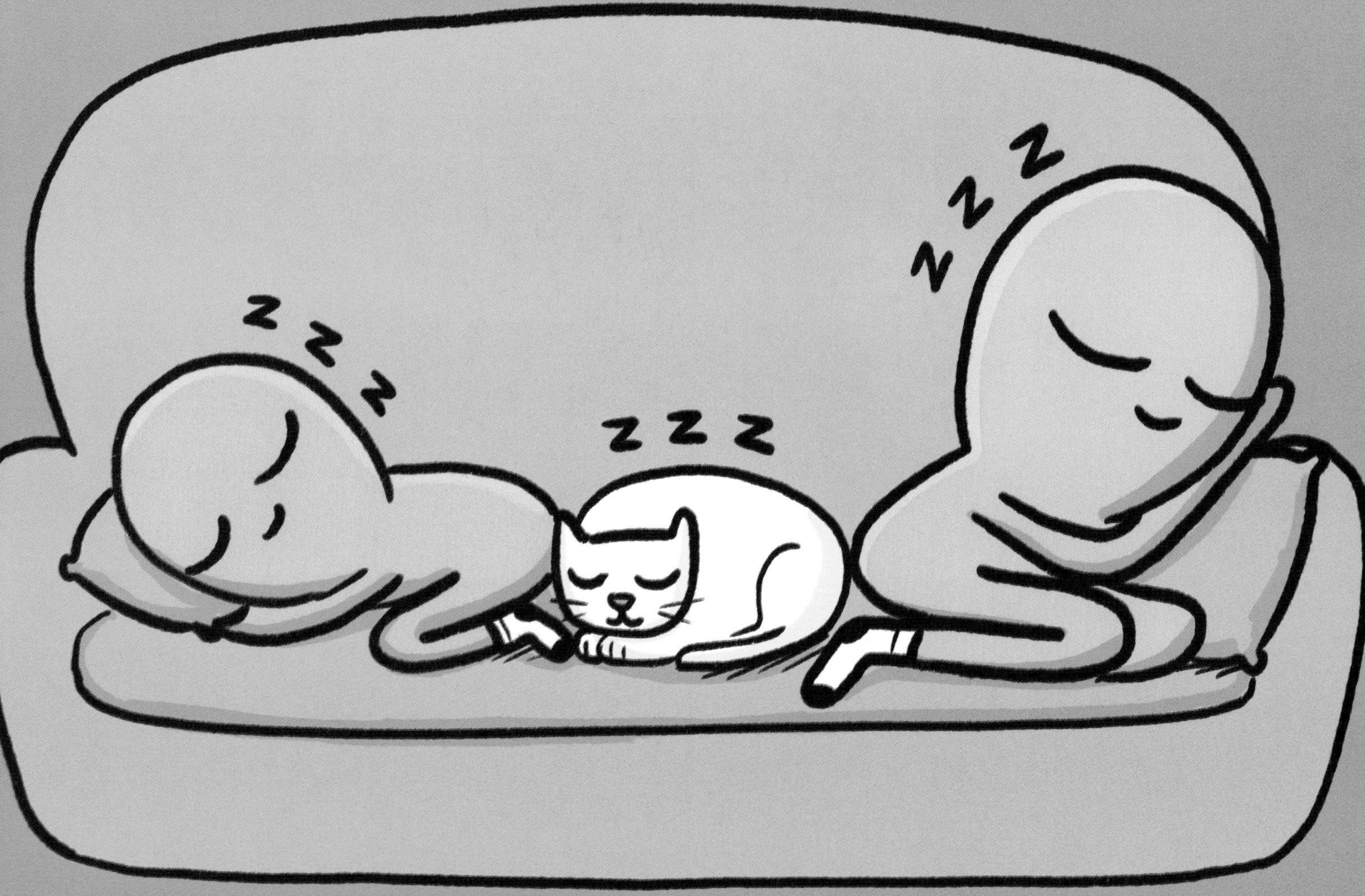

COMMONLY OBSERVED OBJECTS

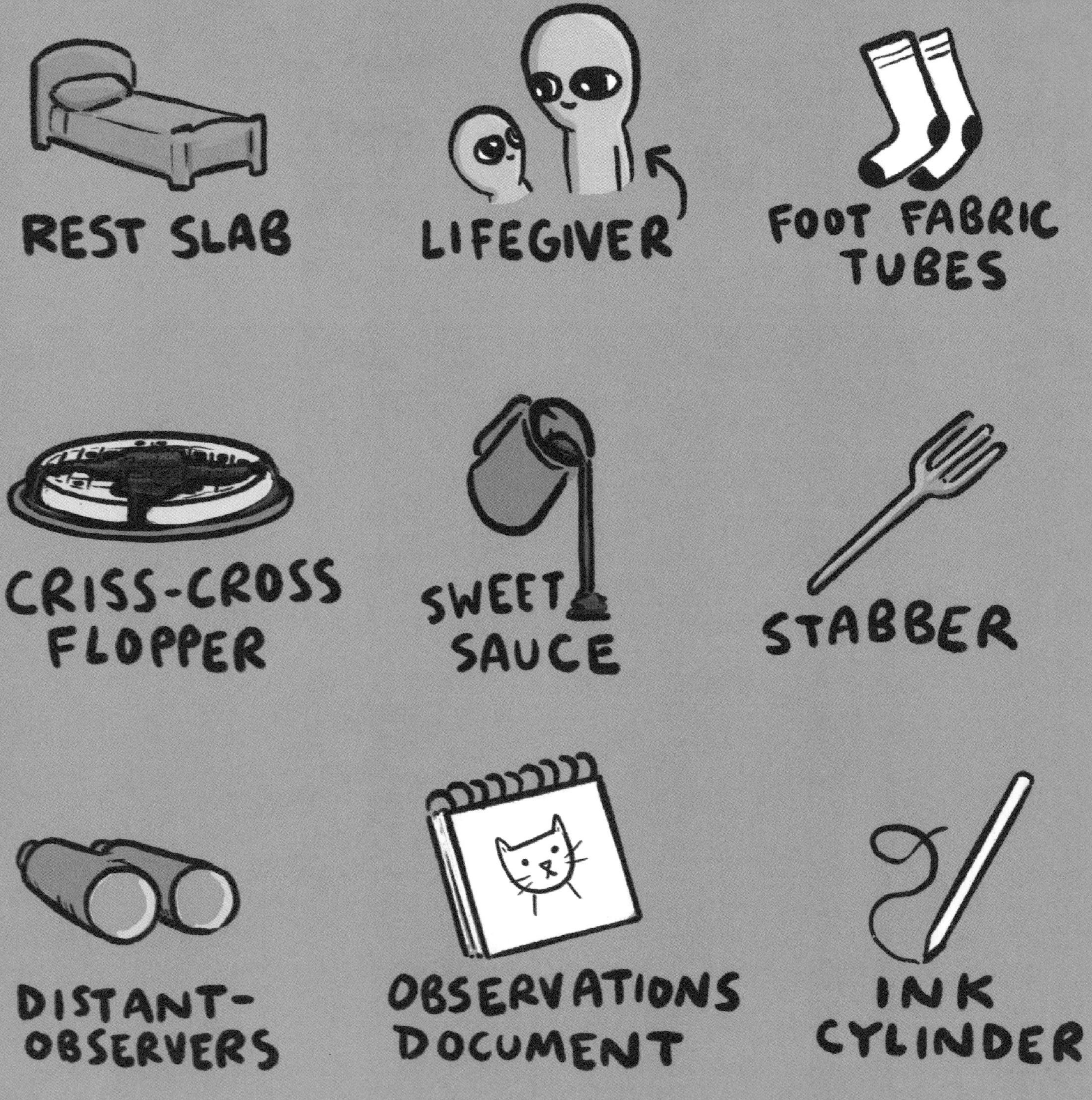

REST SLAB
LIFEGIVER
FOOT FABRIC TUBES
CRISS-CROSS FLOPPER
SWEET SAUCE
STABBER
DISTANT-OBSERVERS
OBSERVATIONS DOCUMENT
INK CYLINDER